Connections

by the Students of Rutherford County

Wax Family Printing, LLC
Murfreesboro, TN

Copyright © 2005 by
Rutherford County Tennessee School System
2240 Southpark Blvd.
Murfreesboro, TN 37128

All rights reserved.
Published by Wax Family Printing, LLC
www.waxfamilyprinting.com

ISBN 0-9726392-9-2 Paperback

Title: Connections, multiple authors.
Subject: Literary Collections, Poetry.

Project Sponsor:
Rutherford County Tennessee Board of Education
Harry Gill, Jr., Director of Schools

Project Coordinators:
Sheila Bratton, Middle Level Coordinator
Elizabeth Church, Language Arts Instructional Specialist
Jackie Drake, Administrative Assistant

For Wax Family Printing:
Publisher: Kevin Wax
Editor: Kevin Wax
Cover Design and Inside Layout: Angel Pardue

Cover Art: Jason Pomeroy, Siegel High School, Grade 11
Back Cover Art: Megan Woolfolk, Riverdale High School, Grade 11
Inside Cover Art: Peyton Milam, Blackman Elementary School, Kindergarten

To publish a book for your school or non-profit organization that complements your academic goals or values, vision and mission, please contact:

Wax Family Printing, LLC
215 MTCS Drive
Murfreesboro, TN 37129

phone: 615-893-4290
fax: 615-893-4295
www.waxfamilyprinting.com

Table of Contents

Introduction/*Harry Gill, Jr.* vii

Chapter One
Connecting through Life's Treasures

Connections/*Melissa Chisum*	3
Artwork by Zachariah Ramsey	3
Greatest Gift/*Callie Lund*	4
Friends are Like Ropes, Tangles and Knots/*Katherine Harber*	4
Two Best Friends/*Chelsey Goode*	4
Valentines Day/*Kim Little*	5
Artwork by Kaylin Davis	5
Nature/*Sydney Cromwell*	6
It is the Time for Gathering/*Donovan Slark*	7
A Bond/*Robert Browning*	7
Hello My Sunshine/*Irieon Walker*	8
Dream World/*William Franklin*	9
A Wagon in a Clover Field/*Rob Wilson*	9
Why I Like Fall/*Olivia Principato*	10
Florida/*Lindon Chastain*	10
The Most Beautiful Thing of All/*Grace Pogue*	10
Hopes of a Snowflake/*Chris Washam*	11
The Lost Baseball Glove/*Brad White*	11
Dreams/*Amy Meyers*	12
Football/*Trevor Woodard*	12
The Warmth of Fall/*Will Kent*	12
My New Pup/*Tommy Gurda*	13
Papa's House/*Keaton Shearron*	13
My Best Friend/*Kayla Sides*	14
Fall's Feast/*Kaci Allison*	14
Our Winter/*Elliot James*	15
My Game/*Michael Medlin*	16
A Fall Morning/*Devin Raines*	16
Fall/*Julia Allen*	17
Thunderstorms/*Amelia Jones*	17
Basketball/*Darius Thompson*	18
Summer Nights/*Nik Mathisen*	18
A Place/*Haley Laney*	19

Hope/*David Stansberry* 19
Soccer/*Cameron Moore* 19
Ocean Breathes Salty/*Kaitlyn Thayvy* 20
The Coal of Fire/*Kristi Bunting* 20
Football Champions/*Justin Hunt* 20
Touchdown/*Matthew Barnes* 21
Baseball/*Adam Pickle* 21
Baseball/*Dylan Townes* 21
Life/*Tim Sandman* 22
Flames/*Amy Shaw* 22
The Day I Found My Cat Symba/*Avery Alsup* 23
What A Hero Is To Me/*Jessica Green* 24
Foster/*Tori Orman* 25
Max/*Lance Leonard* 25
My Dog/*Kelsey Wells* 26
Guitars/*Alexis Fisher* 27
My Gerbil/*Alex Yanovitch* 27
The Dog Next Door/*Amelia Zeller* 27
Being There/*John Meadows* 28
Pride/*Darius Roper* 28
Reema/*Lexi Stacey* 29
Music/*Rondricous Spivey* 29

Chapter Two
Connecting through Personal Thoughts

Hope/*Addison Durham* 33
Change/*Dwight Boshers* 33
World Connections/*Leigh Wilkins* 34
My Life/*Stefan Davenport* 34
All Grown Up/*Koby Jacobs* 34
I Am/*Sharayah Barnes* 35
I Wonder Why, If I/*Kristie Smith* 35
What Is a Connection?/*Anthony Ortiz* 36
Connections/*Dustin Denton* 36
Don't Think You're the Only One/*Morgan Lanza* 37
Step by Step/*Chasity Johnson* 37
Why.../*Logan Garrett* 37
Appreciating/*Elizabeth Henry* 38
Artwork by Dovie Barrett 38

August 13, Journal (Published Posthumously)/*Bruce Gilley* 39
I Hope to Be a Singer/*Lainey Edens* 40
Autumn/*Marisa Jenkins* 40
The People Who Really Count/*Abe Stoklasa* 41
I Am like a Blizzard/*Justin Peery* 42
Life/*Katie Leverette* 42
Always Been a Dream for Me/*Melissa Vickers* 43
Karate/*Elizabeth Pitts* 43
Oh, I Wish I Could Be a Teacher/*Nathan Creech* 44
The Waves/*Elizabeth Ingle* 44
Life Ring/*Robert Johnson* 44
Black and White/*Anthony Myers* 45
The Fight for America/*Robbie Mosley* 45
Threads/*Sarah Riddle* 46
My Dream/*Wesley Parker* 46
Keep These Three/*Matthew Taylor* 46
When I Grow Up/*KaraLynne Levi* 47
Connected?/*Baker Colvert* 47
The Fire Department/*Justin Stile* 47
When I Grow Up/*Alexa Vale* 48
Disconnection/*Graham Overton* 48
I Mite Be a Plesman/*Nathan Luther* 48
Escape the Sounds/*Sarah Rademacher* 49
Horses of the Wild/*Michelle Moore* 49
I Want to be a Vet/*Emily Boone* 49
Rain/*Sarah Hudson* 50
Sports/*Tyler Allen* 50
Raiders/*Taylor Johnson* 51
My Life/*Joshua Greer* 52
Listen/*Molly Guest* 53
Veterans/*Meranda Johnson* 53
What is Love?/*Aimee Albert* 54
If Only.../*Anna Potts* 54
The First Day of School/*Nicole Warrick* 55
Connections/*Tyler Little* 55
Artwork by Macy Swanager 55
I Am Sarah/*Sarah Baker* 56
I Am Unique/*Asha Phillips* 56
I Want to be a Falcons Football Player/*Alex Edens* 56
Dreams/*Taylor Petty* 57

Baseball Is Life/*Caroline Faulkner* 57
Connections/*Mrs. Reta Barney's Class* 57
Back Porch Poet/*Brittney Benton* 58
How Long?/*Angela Rudd* 59
A Friend's Vow/*Amber Stine* 60
Tears/*Thomas Patton* 61
Puzzle Pieces/*Taylor Ezell* 62
Food Fight/*Katie Williams* 62
The School Year/*Kevin Havard* 63
Lawyer/*Spencer Ford* 63
Loved Ones/*Katie Miller* 64
A Dream/*Ethan Floyd* 64
Day/*Rebecca Carden* 64
Butterfly Dance/*Mrs. Sunita Watson's Class* 65
Artwork by Krystin Massa 65
Peer Mentoring/*Rachel La Forte* 66
The Connection/*Jessica Wright* 66
DO MORE/*Ronise Ephord* 67
Dark/*Austin Poteete* 67
I Am/*Kate Simpson* 68
What If/*Rachel La Forte* 69
Scrambled Dreams/*Jessie McMahon* 69
Nature/*Gina Harris* 70
Imagination/*Sarah Farris* 71
Do You Ever?/*Keela Fults* 71
This World of Ours/*Danielle Aroujo* 71
Today/*Hannan Creasey* 72
The Dreamer/*Deborah Anderson* 72
The Best Angel/*Matthew Goodman* 73
Connecting/*Katie Gardner* 74
Artwork by Cristina Brito 74
3:43/*Elizabeth Hooper* 75
Autumn/*Jordan Mingis* 76
Where People Can Connect/*Ella Strawman* 76
Fall in the Air/*Tyler Brooks* 77
Chains/*Carly Davis* 78
Artwork by Brady Seymore 78

Chapter Three
Connecting through Fond Memories

I Remember/*Skyler Holder* 81
First Football Game/*Matthew Bohannon* 81
I Remember/*Sonny Yang* 81
Christmas/*Caitlin Cheadle* 82
Memories/*Danielle Vincion* 82
Victory/*Jessica Blankenship* 83
The Buzzer Beater/*Peyton Motroni* 83
My Favorite Memory/*Dakota Smith* 84
A Raggedy Ann/*Allison Anderson* 84
My Favorite Memory/*Desirae Parrish* 84
Homeroom King/*Parker Burgess* 84
My Favorite Memories/*Paige Gronbach* 85
Movie Memory/*Tanner Nokes* 85
My Football Game/*Dejuan Martin* 85
One December Morning/*Tristan Rush* 86
Artwork by Danielle Burr 86
Memories/*Tucker Webb* 87
James Island, South Carolina/*Jacob Richardson* 88
Cookie Day/*Shannon Aderholt* 88
My Grandfather's Words/*Phillip Dodd* 89
Tumbling Down the Stairs/*Daniel Warren* 90
Connection Rejection/*Kalen Johnson* 91
Memories of Childhood/*Sarah Schott* 91
Connections/*Mikayla Mityok* 92
Snow Day/*Kayla Goyette* 92
Sweet, Sweet Memories/*Victoria Torres* 93
Walt Disney World/*Bethany* 93
I Had My Birthday Party/*Nash Vinkler* 93
Memories/*Emily Wood* 94
Friday Nights!/*Sam Douglas* 94
Thanksgiving/*Damien Alcorn* 94
My Trip To Destin/*Tommi Abernathy* 95
Thanksgiving/*Cody Blankenship* 95
Thanksgiving/*Audrey McAteer* 95
My Trip to the Beach/*Sidney Baker* 95
Bluebird/*Kaley Stroup* 96
A Fun Beach Trip/*Jazmin Scheitel* 96
Picture of Hope/*Sophie Boehm* 96

Going to the Zoo/*Nicholas Mazzella* 96
Melissa/*Rachel Rounion* 97
On the Beach/*Kelsey Young* 98
I Remember/*Karl Luboniecki* 99
A Special Memory/*Kolby Frazier* 100
A Special Holiday/*Ben Godwin* 100
The Wedding Day/*Dianna Bartilson* 100
I Can Still Remember/*Allison Keener* 101
When I Grow Up/*Shelby Langford*..101
My Brother!/*Autumn Harris*...101
Belle Aire/*Sam Loyd*...102
Artwork by Autumn Jones 102
To Stacey/*Jacob S. VanEkelenburg*...103
My Cat/*Caroline Wells* 104
Daddy's Girl/*Amy Graham* 104
Christmas/*Chad Perkins* 105
The Beach/*Abigail Phonygamy* 105
My Cousin's Baby Brother/*Samuel Pitts* 105
Memories/*Autumn Campbell* 106
My First Christmas/*Rosanny Brito*..106
The Sound of Laughter/*Kaitlin Beck* 107
Reflections/*Johnathan Mullins*...108
About My Seventh Birthday/*Alexandra Cunfidd* 109
The Best Ball Game/*Tyler Beck* 109
My First Christmas/*Lexus Saunders*...109
Baseball/*Kinley Seaborn*...109
My Favorite Memory/*Crawford Swafford* 110
A Wonderful Place/*Emily Summers* 110

Chapter Four
Connecting through Family Memories

My Special Family/*Brock Baker*..113
Connection Flag/*Logan Coffey*..114
Daddy/*Mary Katherine Bogle* 114
Holiday Cheer/*Kayleigh Barnes*..114
Family/*Harris Smith* 115
I Love My Uncle/*Kyle Herndon* 115
Family/*Ashley Stanton* 116
The Best Mommy/*Victoria Alexander* 116

Wrapped in Your Arms/*Ukeye Wilt* 117
My New Baby Sister/*Christopher Patton* 117
Impact/*Lisa Calabrese* 118
My Hero, My Grandfather/*William Gaines* 118
My Sister Maddy/*Chelsea Williams* 119
Connections/*Shawn Cannon* 120
Why!/*Zach Ritter* 120
My Brother and Me/*Kacee Pieratt* 120
In Loving Memory of Daddy/*Mandy Reeves* 121
My Little Brother/*Tyler Bouttavong* 121
And I Remember/*Jessica Shelkey* 122
Connection to My Grandpa/*Cass Jones* 123
God Just Couldn't Resist Her/*Amy Cochran* 123
My Grandpa and I/*Roxanna Bustillo* 123
My Mama/*Isaac Haley* 124
My Dad/*Rodney Schade* 124
Dad/*Adrianna Moss* 124
How I Became a Chef/*Billie Daniella Walden* 125
David, My Brother, My Hero/*Zachary Green* 125
My Childhood/*Mallory Pawlik* 125
Thank You/*Chelsa Read* 126
Appreciation/*Angela Leyhew* 126
Dear Brother/*Leanna McClintock* 127
My Dad is Special/*Jaylee Oliver* 127
My Grandma/*Cody West* 127
A Special Time/*Kirstin Taylor* 128
My Brother Grayson/*Taylor Rigsby* 128
My Special Person/*Trey McAdams* 128
Thank You, Jim/*Dustin Mears* 129
The Mother's Day Plate/*MaryGrace Bouldin* 129
Mother Deary/*Nicky Balduf* 129
My Baby Sister/*Kristen Barnes* 130
My Family/*Julia Durant* 130
My Twin Brothers/*Zachary Fussell* 130
My Grandpa/*Patrick Stanford* 130
I Am/*Ashley Thompson* 131
Grandmother/*Mayra Campusano* 131
My Family/*Brendan Willis* 132
My Mom/*Eli Clutter* 132
Uncle/*Caroline Love* 132
Grammy and Grampa/*Caitlin Meier* 133

Mother/*Austin Roden* 133
When I Go with Papa/*Allie Nadeau* 133
Aubrey's Family/*Aubrey Kinney* 134
My Family/*Kaitlyn Palmer* 134
A Special Person/*Amanad Pratt* 134
My Last Family Christmas Memory/*Misty Davenport* 135
All About Mom/*Ethan Young* 136
I Remember Grandpa/*Ashley Wise* 136
Remember When/*Tangelia Cannon* 137
Sister Poem/*Levi Morales* 139
Connections like a Magnet/*Logan Caffrey* 139
Special One/*Kate Walrath* 140
My Great-grandma/*Cole Woodward* 140
The Girl Next Door/*Katie Shacklett* 141
Family and Friends/*Keira Biggs* 141
My Brother/*Morgan Taylor* 142
She's Here/*Kaitlin Hurt* 142
Daddy/*Chase McBryar* 142
Twins/*Chad Russell/Chris Russell* 143
Artwork by Kelsey Dearmon 143
My Mom/*Erin Paul* 144
Maddie/*Brittany Smith* 145
Loved One/*Penn Moore* 145
My Mother/*Jeavonna Coble* 146
Hero/*Blake Adams-Manuel* 146
I Believe I Can Fly/*Kalie L. Davis* 146
Mom/*Kalie Boyer* 147
Family Traditions/*Joey Meier* 147
That Was For Grandpa/*Justine Mettler* 148
Times Spent with Grandma/*Michael Pethke* 148
Clean Clothes/*Brett Bloom* 149
Something I Did in Japan/*Yoshimi Kajisa* 149
Granny/*Ally Eaton* 150
Love and Limitations/*Kelsey Caffy* 150

RUTHERFORD COUNTY BOARD OF EDUCATION

Harry Gill, Jr., Director of Schools

2240 Southpark Boulevard
Murfreesboro, Tennessee 37128
Phone (615) 893-5812   Fax (615) 898-7940

February 14, 2005

Dear Reader,

With this book, <u>Connections</u>, the students of Rutherford County once again reveal their talents both artistically and with the written word. This is the sixth in a series of outstanding works from our students. They inspire us to connect to our own fond remembrances, family memories, and life's treasures.

Each student's connection shares a special time, person, or memory that evokes deep feelings. For Taylor Ezell it is the realization of how each piece of the puzzle of life is a connection to our future; for Callie Lund it is the importance of the strong connection between friends; and for Kalen Johnson it is the irony of a connection rejection.

As you read, I invite you to reflect upon your own thoughts and memories that lift your spirit and make connections in your life.

Best regards,

Harry Gill

Harry Gill, Jr.
Director of Schools

Moving Beyond Excellence

Chapter One

Connecting through Life's Treasures

Connections
Melissa Chisum
Blackman Middle School, Grade 6

Coming together with family and friends
Overcoming fears
New beginnings each morning
New people to meet every day
Expressing your feelings
Creating something to make life better
Taking time to notice the small things in life
Inching towards a better way
Opening new doors
Never giving up
Seeing and learning new things every day

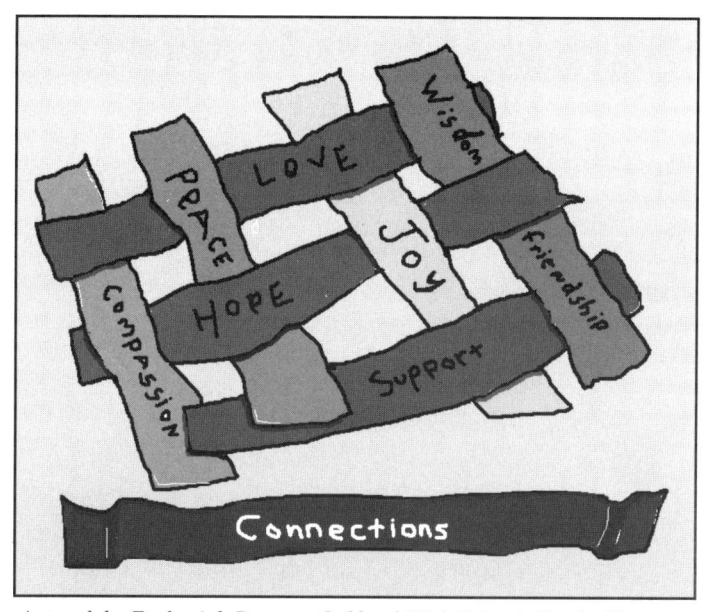

Artwork by Zachariah Ramsey, Oakland High School, Grade 12

Greatest Gift
Callie Lund
Oakland High School, Grade 11

Loyalty
Exists in friends,
Creates a bond.
It is a connection that cannot be broken.
Cherish it;
It is the greatest gift that can be given.

Friends Are like Ropes, Tangles, and Knots
Katherine Harber
Thurman Francis Arts Academy, Grade 5

Friends are like ropes, sturdy and straight
Some are so perfect...they never ever break.
Then there's a few that go in an angle
They get so bad that they turn into tangles.
Knots are the worst....they always stay
And if you're not careful they'll never go away.
So be smart and cherish these friendship dates
Then your ropes will be sturdy and straight.

Two Best Friends
Chelsey Goode
Blackman Elementary School, Grade 3

Two best friends are loyal it's true,
They never leave each other no matter what they go through,
They hold each other up when they feel blue,
Through the good times,
the bad times,
even though they don't know what to do,
Two best friends are the best thing it's true,
I'm so glad I have a best friend…
                         just …
                                 like…
                                         you!

Valentine's Day
Kim Little
Siegel Middle School, Grade 8

>It is almost here
>When hearts and flowers are sent
>That special time of year
>Sent by the hours from people who care
>Brought to all who seek
>When kisses swirl
>Words do peak into cotton candy
>My heart whirls.
>
>So be my own love
>Send me a card
>Call me on the phone
>That is not hard to do
>Come see me by my waiting door
>And I will be yours forever more.

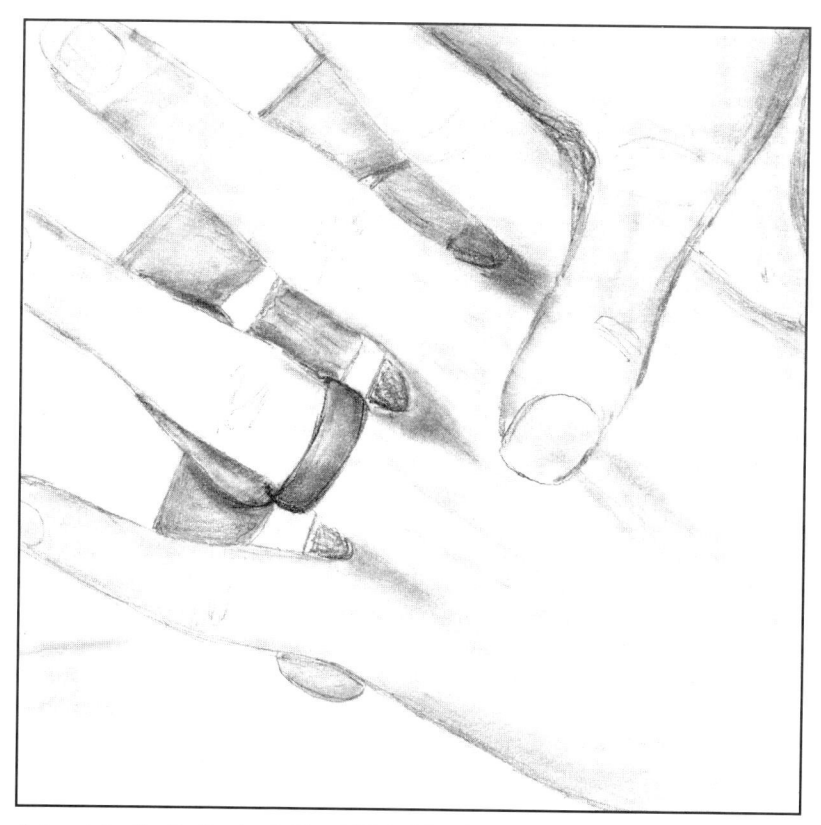

Artwork by Kaylin Davis, Oakland High School, Grade 12

Nature

Sydney Cromwell
McFadden School of Excellence, Grade 6

As I walk along the sun-dappled path,
With leafy oak trees over my head,
And moist, rocky soil under my feet,
There is peace and contentment where I tread.

Birds twitter in happy harmony,
Squirrels dash to and fro,
A buck stares at me for a moment
Then dashes away with a quick, graceful doe.

I finally reach my destination,
A pond in the middle of the forest,
Where frogs, insects, fish, and more
Set up a sweet-sounding chorus.

I sit there for a while,
Just glad to get away,
From all the trials, trouble, and heartbreak
A person must deal with every day.

Finally, I begin my walk
Back to the cul-de-sac.
But one thing is certain,
I will definitely be back.

It is the Time for Gathering
Donavan Slark
Cedar Grove Elementary School, Grade 4

Thank you for all my hands can hold;
A knife to carve the turkey,
A bow in my hand and the feel of letting the arrow go,
A book in my hand,
A plate for my food.

Thank you for all my eyes can see;
The yellow moon in the night-black sky,
The brown, hot turkey on the table,
My family at the table,
Presents for my father on his birthday.

Thank you for all my ears can hear;
Crunchy leaves on my socks,
Whistling in the wind,
My little puppy in the leaves and barking,
Laughter at the table.

It is the time for gathering.

A Bond
Robert Browning
Thurman Francis Arts Academy, Grade 8

A bond
A connection between two people
A warm and fuzzy feeling
A truth
A living emotion
A way of life
A thing that stays right forever
Always constant, never ending cycle
Love

Hello My Sunshine
Irieon Walker
Smyrna High School, Grade 11

I wake up full of energy, charged, and ready to start my day.
But I still need another boost to get me on my way.

I look to my window, and I see the closed blinds from the last day.
I could see the sunrays peering through each and every crack.
So I reach out for the twirling wand that rotates my blinds ajar and take a peak at what lies ahead of me in the world today.

For a second, the sunlight is blazing at my eyes.
Then the morning rays touch my check with a kiss.
The light touches my skin and brings out its true,
full, and rich caramel color.

She comes gently into my room and
engulfs all that was once dark and gloom.
The infectious color and feel of her brightness force me to smile.
I can hear her say deep down inside of me
"Are you ready to tackle the day, my child?"
That single feeling soothes my body and washes my fears away.

Now I have that extra boost.
I can make it through another blessed, God-given day.

I will jump hurdles thrown my way.
Will do it just the way my family teaches me to each and every day.

Dream World
William Franklin
Thurman Francis Arts Academy, Grade 6

There is a place we go to every night
We can walk, run, or take a flight.
No matter how we get there, as long as we come
It gives us a chance to meet every one.
In this place you can ride a rubber dinosaur
Or be friends with a *wild* boar.
You can ride down a golden stream
Then wake up and wonder…was it all a dream?

A Wagon in a Clover Field
Rob Wilson
Christiana Middle School, Grade 8

In this period of time, we think only of our problems
    and misfortunes,
But not of what we do have or what we can achieve
Sometimes we should look at the simple things and enjoy what
    they bring
Like an old red wagon in a carpet of clover
Clover flowing throughout the hillside.

I wonder
Was it fun rolling in that wagon?
As I look at the abandoned wagon, I realize its work is done.
This stays on my mind.
I want people to see this wagon, to really see it.
In the meantime, I'll go back to the world of problems;
I'll forget what beauty really is.
That was my red wagon.

Why I Like Fall
Olivia Principato
Walter Hill Elementary School, Kindergarten

I like fall because I like to jump in the leaves and my cat Cosmo jumps with me.

Florida
Lindon Chastain
Lascassas Elementary School, Grade 5

Fun in the sun at the beach
␣Love building sandcastles
Orange juice every morning
Rain hardly ever comes
It's your everyday paradise
Disneyland is always awesome
Always use sunscreen.

The Most Beautiful Thing of All
Grace Pogue
McFadden School of Excellence, Grade 5

As time flies by
I look into the night
And wonder at the beauty in everyday life.
When the bird cracks open the now empty shell
When the leaves turn from a jungle vine green to pumpkin-orange
When the tiny tiger cub becomes a fierce predator
When all of these things change
I change with them.
Until I grow older and wiser
Until my children and grandchildren
Look out beyond the skyscrapers and airplanes
And onto just a field of wheat
And notice that it is the most beautiful thing of all.

Hopes of a Snowflake
Chris Washam
LaVergne Middle School, Grade 7

Snowflakes gliding through the air
Falling carefully without a care.

Filling the trees with a white hint
Never stopping their decent.

Putting on an elegant show
Falling on a blanket of snow.

The Lost Baseball Glove
Brad White
Wilson Elementary School, Grade 3

One day I had a game against the Braves when I was playing at Leanna. When it was over, I had to get out of the dugout because another team was coming in to play a game. The next day I noticed I was missing my glove. Later in the day I went to the ball fields to start hunting for my glove. First, I asked Lost and Found if they had it, but they didn't have it. Next, my mom and dad called my coach, but he wasn't available. A couple of hours later we were back home. We called again, and my mom talked to him about my glove. He said, "Sorry. You guys might need a new one." First we went to Old Navy to begin a new search. Next we went to Grand Slam. We bought a glove from them. When we went home we faced a bigger challenge. It's called working the glove so you can close it. We still had one problem – getting through kid pitch. By the end of the season I had mastered the glove. People still say it was my best season ever.

Dreams
Amy Meyers
Oakland High School, Grade 9

Drift through the
Ripples of our mind
Enable our imagination to wander
Act as a place to
Make a perfect
Stratosphere of peace.

Football
Trevor Woodard
Walter Hill Elementary School, Grade 2

Football in the air
Ow! that hurts
Oh! another touchdown
Touchdown
Bright lights
After the game
Loud crowd
Little guy running.

The Warmth of Fall
Will Kent
Blackman Middle School, Grade 7

The warmth of fall
The leaves of heat
Orange, yellow, red,
crunching under my feet.

The stars in the sky
Showing me the path,
But the shadow of the fire
Won't let me through,
So I look for the summer
for a good star's view.

My New Pup
Tommy Gurda
Blackman Elementary School, Grade 3

I was so happy to get a pup.
He was cute. He was cuddly.
But he would hardly get up!
I was worried for my pet,
So I took him to the vet.
He was sick.
It was ick.
He had worms!

Papa's House
Keaton Shearron
McFadden School of Excellence, Grade 8

There is a place where I can go.
It's far away from here,
Separated by miles of highway…
But close to my heart.

> Visions of long green grass
> Whipping around a little girl's legs,
> Separated by years of growth…
> But still in my memories.

There is a place I'm always welcome,
Where warmth surrounds me like a blanket.
Separated by the routine of everyday life…
But always waiting for my return.

> Visions of arms embracing,
> Wrapping around a little girl's heart,
> Separated only by time…
> But always present in my dreams.

There is a place where I can go.
It's far away from here,
Separated by miles and time…
But connected forever to the little girl who lives in me.

My Best Friend
Kayla Sides
Blackman Elementary School, Grade 5

One sunny Easter morning
The Easter bunny came.
In my den he left me
The one who would become my best friend.

He was blue with floppy ears,
Bright eyes, and a knowing smile
Somehow I knew he was special
And he would be with me for a long, long while.

Fall's Feast
Kaci Allison
Blackman Middle School, Grade 7

Sensing the warmness of all the reds, browns, oranges, and golds
Like mama's sweet apple pie
One bite and you're sold.

Locks and curls blowing round from the fall air
Just like Daddy's fingers
Running through my hair.

I see those leaves fall to the ground
Like when the family eats merrily
That flaky piecrust that falls into an applesauce mound.

The wind outside gathers all the leaves big and small
Like my Aunt May getting the family together
The old, the young, the plump, the flat, the short and the tall.

Every year this season is held at the same place
Like every year we sit down
Say God bless, and finish the grace.

Our Winter

Elliot James
Siegel High School, Grade 10

This is my winter.
The time when frozen breath mingled,
Brings me back to the time of you and me.
When the sounds of crunching ice beneath
Cold feet were so familiar to our ears. When
We could pick up the petrified leaves of autumn
And toss them into the streets, watching as
They fell almost as slow as the snow. It
Reminded me of how gently your beautiful
Hair fell to your shoulders.

This is your winter, also.
The time when frozen memories form as
Sparkling icicles in our minds, sticking as
Long as our love was here. The time when
Grey clouds of frost would gather in your
Eyes, showing your worries and troubles for
Me and only me. We could sit for hours,
Knowing we had our hopes, our pasts, our
Futures, our winter. Together.

This is our winter.

My Game
Michael Medlin
Blackman Elementary School, Grade 5

Whether I'm at the field or
At home, I'm still thinking about
It. I'm either watching or playing football.

I love how the quarterback
Throws the ball.
Or, how the
Running back runs with it.

Every Saturday I go to my game
Whether it's early or late.

Now my season is over and
I'm ready to start back really soon.

A Fall Morning
Devin Raines
Blackman Middle School, Grade 7

A fall morning, sun shining through the red, orange sky. Golden leaves blowing onto the ground. Birds making a creep-creep sound. Tall green glass blowing making a swoosh sound. People making crushing sounds as they walk through the leaves. Kids laughing as they head to school. Moms and dads slamming doors, trying not to be late for work. Infants crying, not wanting to be left with a babysitter. But I stand there in the driveway thinking how small I am now in this big world. How peaceful and happy I am to walk out of my house on this fall morning.

Fall
Julia Allen
Blackman Elementary School, Grade 3

Crinkle, crinkle,

Crunch, crunch,

Leaves for the deer to munch.

There are children

Playing dolls and ball,

People going to the mall,

All enjoying

The wonderful weather of fall.

Thunderstorms
Amelia Jones
Blackman Middle School, Grade 7

A cloudy sky
before bed
the wind is blowing
telling me a storm is coming.
The rain starts pouring.
I hear it trickle on my window.
It thunders loudly
and I am scared.
Lightening fills the sky.
I run into my mother's room.
The rain pours down harder.
She holds me tight.
The rain softens;
the lightening and the thunder stop.
I fall asleep.

Basketball

Darius Thompson
Blackman Elementary School, Grade 4

B is for basketball, the best sport I ever played.
A is for awesome and so cool to play.
S is for swish when you score without touching the rim.
K is for keeping up when you're guarding your man.
E is for excellent and fun to play.
T is for two teams playing against each other.
B is for bouncing the ball up and down the court.
A is for attitude so you can have fun.
L is learning new things.
L is for listen to your coach.

Summer Nights

Nik Mathisen
Eagleville High School, Grade 11

Sitting on the front porch hearing Mother Nature's orchestra sing to us

As a slow, rolling thunderstorm rolls by.

Lighting up the sky like a display of fireworks,

Feeling the warmth of summer wrapping itself around me,

Having a light breeze comb through my hair,

Seeing the lightning bugs flying themselves into a fury

Looking like a thousand shooting stars.

That is when I know that summer is upon me.

A Place
Haley Laney
Blackman Elementary School, Grade 4

When sunshine lights up my face
I think about a place.
A place where there's sand
And water splashes my hand.
Where the ocean is so deep
You'd never fall asleep.
When the waves crash the shore
You'll be wanting more.
This place is the beach.
I love it more then a peach.

Hope
David Stansberry
McFadden School of Excellence, Grade 6

     My hopes are very important to my life. They tell me what I hope to be, what I hope to have, and how I hope to feel. I think hopes are important to everybody, because their effects are all around us.

     What if George Washington never hoped to be in the army, and the British had won the Revolutionary War? What if Martin Luther King, Jr. had never hoped to be a public speaker and had never given other people hope?

     How do you think anybody ever became successful? They hoped and dreamed. Then they followed those hopes and dreams. My hopes are very simple; they are to have success and happiness. My opinion is, if you have those two things and people who love you, you don't need anything else.

Soccer
Cameron Moore
Blackman Elementary School, Grade 5

Racing to the goal
Sweat running down my face
Wind blowing like it's
Helping me dribble the ball.
I'm going so fast it feels
Like I am flying over the grass,
But when I shoot the ball,
It seems like everything stops.
But then it goes in and everything
Gets fired back up and
It feels so good; it's great!

Ocean Breathes Salty

Kaitlyn Thayvy
Blackman Middle School, Grade 7

Ocean breathes salty,
On the warm beach;
Sun shining brightly,
Hot-dogs fifty cents each.

Ocean breathes salty,
Castles in the sand,
Swimming in the ocean,
Crabs pinching free hands.

The Coal of the Fire

Kristi Bunting
Oakland High School, Grade 11

The home-fires burn with steady flames.
A sacrifice has been laid upon the altar.
The burnt offering, a soldier, the source of our energy,
Having fought, has died with loyalty and honor.

Football Champions

Justin Hunt
Smyrna Primary School, Grade 5

Different city
Different football field
Score tied
Made a tackle
Made a touchdown
Bulldogs won!
We are the champions!
Greatest day of my life!
Party at my house.

Touchdown
Matthew Barnes
Blackman Elementary School, Grade 4

> I'm running down the field.
> I'm not running on my heels.
> As I'm rocking down the field.
> The turf starts to peel.
> My legs are getting tired,
> But I'm not giving up.
> Then I'll take a big jump.
> TOUCHDOWN!!!

Baseball
Adam Pickle
Smyrna Primary School, Grade 4

Hit, run, catch, slide
Helmet, ball, bat, glove
Single, double, triple, homerun
First base, second base, third base, home
Batter, catcher, pitcher, shortstop
Happy, energetic, tense, nervous
Hard work, fun, team, sport.

I love baseball!!

Baseball
Dylan Townes
Thurman Francis Arts Academy, Grade 3

Baseball, baseball
Oh how I love baseball.
I dream of it,
I play it,
And I know it.
I love baseball,
Oh yeah!

Life
Tim Sandman
Oakland High School, Grade 11

                Life is a gift,
        Given only to those who survive.
            Miraculously created,
          In a loving mother's womb.

Flames
Amy Shaw
Oakland High School, Grade 11

Soldiers are flames
Burning with honor and hope
Bravely opposing
The cold.

The Day I Found My Cat Symba

Avery Alsup
Wilson Elementary School, Grade 4

"Mama, can I please have a cat?" I asked. She told me to ask Santa, but I told her that I wanted nothing for Christmas but an orange cat. Two weeks before Christmas, the TV was on and then we heard this awful noise. It sounded like cats fighting!

We opened the door an inch or two, and this little orange kitten, that looked like it was starving, walked in. I gave him milk and tuna, and he drank and ate every bit. He was so cute! So I called my daddy to ask if I could keep him.

"Daddy, I found this kitten, and he's so cute. Can I keep him?"

"Guess what," he said. "Put him back out, and if he's there in the morning you can keep him."

Excited, I hung up. To make sure he would still be there in the morning, I put out milk, ham, and an old wool blanket.

The next day my daddy came home from work, and as we opened the door we discovered he wasn't there. I started to sob, just then my brother said, "I see Kitty!"

I ran to see, and there he was under a chair. I picked him up, and he was purring very loudly. I brought him inside.

"Can we keep him?" I asked.

"Yes, but does he have fleas?" Daddy responded.

We checked behind his ears, and he did have fleas but that didn't stop me from hugging him. I sat him down, and he ran everywhere. He even jumped on and off our beds.

Later that day, I went with my mom to get cat food, a litter box, and toys. When we got home, I put the litter in the litter box. The next day we took him to the vet to get him flea-free. He wasn't happy, but he forgave us.

Everything went well with my cat, Symba, we decided to name him that because he looks like Symba from the <u>Lion King</u>. Other than getting him potty trained and keeping him off the kitchen table, all has gone smoothly. I got my Christmas wish, and Symba got a home.

What a Hero Is to Me
Jessica Green
Smyrna High School, Grade 11

What makes someone a hero?
It's nothing really new,
It's something deep inside of you,
The leader coming through.

You may not consider yourself
But you may very well be
A leader, a winner,
For all the world to see.

We read about heroes all the time,
And see them on T.V.
They have flashy names like Superman
With x-ray eyes to see.

But how about some other guys,
Who aren't printed in our books?
They haven't got the flashy suits
Or looks of a hero.

Now out of all my heroes
Not one can crash through walls,
They have no x-ray vision,
And they don't stand ten feet tall.

But all of them are heroes,
Their actions speak louder than their words.
They are there for you
Both through the good and bad times.

Your hero may be the one that saved you
Or the one that you look up to.
Or your hero may be just like my hero,
Your closest friend!

Foster
Tori Orman
Walter Hill Elementary School, Grade 1

Foster was my dog. He was a very good dog. Foster always did what I wanted him to do. He was a grayish color. I am sad because Foster died. I miss him very much.

Max
Lance Leonard
Lascassas Elementary School, Grade 5

My dog Max
Enjoyable, energetic
Monsterously massive
Obviously obedient
Really rowdy
Incredibly intelligent
Extremely excellent
Super Superlative

My Dog
Kelsey Wells
Thurman Francis Arts Academy, Grade 8

I love my dog,
He is special to me,
After reading this poem,
You'll be able to see.

While I was still sleeping
One December day,
My dad was reading the paper
In his usual way.

Then he saw an ad
For a basset hound,
A puppy that needed a home,
Or else to the pound he'd go.

So we went to the house,
Where he was to be sold,
He was on the porch,
Shivering in the cold.

There he was sleeping
On brown paper sacks,
So we brought him home,
And we named him Max.

I think we've trained him well,
He knows just what to do,
But he sometimes gets excited,
And chews on a shoe.

He knows how to fetch,
He'll run and play all day,
When I come home from school,
He greets me in his slobbery way.

Max is very happy,
We love him all to death,
And he loves us too.
I think he is the best!

Guitars
Alexis Fisher
Walter Hill Elementary School, Grade 1

Guitars are taking time to learn and play. But you have to take lessons to learn how to play and get good at a guitar. But I like to play guitars because you will learn very good at it. Because the more you learn, the more you get very good at it. But you have to play very, very much more to get better and better at it. You will learn about it if you keep on learning it just the way you will learn.

My Gerbil
Alex Yanovitch
Thurman Francis Arts Academy, Grade 2

I have had my gerbil for two days.
He is a very, very, good gerbil.
I wish I could always be right next to him. Close, dear friends we are!
No matter how far away from each other, we'll always feel we're together.
I love him and care for him much, much, much more than a pet or friend.
I care for him like the dearest part of the family.

The Dog Next Door
Amelia Zeller
Walter Hill Elementary School, Grade 1

The dog next door licks my face. He is really funny. I like the dog next door. I like to play with him. When I play with him, he gets excited. The dog next door is really friendly.

Being There
John Meadows
Oakland High School, Grade 10

"Connection" is being in a new school when nobody knows you, but you make a new friend. It's when you are having a bad day and someone reaches out to you because they've been there. It's when you see someone in need and you help them, because you've been there. It's being there always. Friendship is the connection.

Pride
Darius Roper
Siegel High School, Grade 11

Teasing tan and a paper sack brown,
That is my skin color,
For which I am sometimes put down.

But the color of my skin is not my fault,
But a thing called PRIDE
Is what I have been taught.

This thing called PRIDE,
Is an awesome wonder.
This is what keeps my head
From going under.

Reema

Lexi Stacey
Lascassas Elementary School, Grade 5

My best friend
Enjoys playing with me
Most of the time
Outside at
Recess.
I think of her
Everywhere including
School.

Music

Rondricous Spivey
Oakland High School, Grade 10

Music is the connection to our souls.
No matter how sick, healthy, young or old,
The rhythm is connected to my heartbeat,
Which controls the movement to my feet.
Music joins all people together.
Music will be a major part of my life forever.

Chapter Two
Connecting through Personal Thoughts

Hope
Addison Durham
Thurman Francis Arts Academy, Grade 5

> Hope for a good thing,
> Whatever it might bring.
>
> Hope for a good thing,
> It just might ring.
>
> Hope for a good thing,
> That's all I have to say.
>
> Hope for a good thing,
> It might come a mile away!

Change
Dwight Boshers
LaVergne Middle School, Grade 7

I was a liar.
I was a cheat.
I was a fake, with no heartbeat.
I was a loser, with no reputation.
I was a freak that couldn't appreciate a conversation.
I was a sunk-in kind of guy.
I made bad decisions, but I didn't know why.
I was feeling down and low.
That was a long time ago.
Now I am better, rearranged.
I did something a lot of people should do…
I changed.

World Connections
Leigh Wilkins
Oakland High School, Grade 12

Muscles and bones connect to make you.
Hearts and minds make us up too.
Bricks connect to make a home.
Words connect to make a poem.

Wires connect to make a call.
A batter swings to connect with a ball.
Noises connect to make a sound.
There are different connections all around!

My Life
Stefan Davenport
Blackman Middle School, Grade 6

As I sit in this summer breeze,
I wonder about my parents, the divorcees.
Some people think it's no big deal,
But I wonder if my inner scars will ever heal.

All Grown Up
Koby Jacobs
Wilson Elementary School, Grade 1

I would like to be a nurse when I grow up. I like to help people. I would make sure they are safe. I will give them a shot to make sure they feel better. Also, I will get them a wheel chair so they can move around.

I Am

Sharayah Barnes
Rock Springs Middle School, Grade 7

I am who I am
I wonder why some people can't accept that
I hear my "friends" talking behind my back
I see my "friends" ignoring me
I want to be accepted as me
I am who I am.

I pretend to be someone I'm not
I believe in others, but they don't believe in me
I feel bad when someone betrays me
I worry that I'm not good enough
I cry myself to sleep some nights
I am who I am.

I understand when someone feels the same way
I say it doesn't bug me, but it does
I love those who are loyal to our relationship
I am who I am.

I Wonder Why, If I

Kristie Smith
Smyrna West Alternative School, Grade 7

I wonder why they made a sky.
To give you something to look at when we start to cry?
If I were a bird, which way would I fly? And why?
If I had a clone, would I like to be around it?
If I were in someone else's shoes, would I like it better?
If I had three wishes, would I wish for something stupid or more wishes?
If I had a problem, would I tell?
If I could change my entire life, would I?

What Is a Connection?
Anthony Ortiz
McFadden School of Excellence, Grade 7

"What is a connection?" you ask.
When a little girl holds her dolly dear,
When a small boy holds his teddy bear,
When one can never be separated with an object,
A connection is bonding.

When a man is twenty and his mother will still cuddle him,
When she will still rock him to sleep,
When she will still sing in a soft voice to make him sleep,
A connection is that special place in a mother's heart that never goes away.

When a kid can tell his schoolmate anything and the person will understand,
When a boy can lean his head on a needed shoulder in times of pain and despair,
When a child desperately needs a friend and none but a single person will be one,
A connection is the deepest and truest form of friendship one will ever find.

Connections
Dustin Denton
LaVergne Middle School, Grade 7

The lights in my heart
grow brighter by the minute.

Looking to my past
remembering everyone in it.

The ones that are here
the ones that came and passed.

All the love we shared
never can go bad.

The hard times came
and the good times came a many.

We all still share
the light and love within.

All of us saying
the connections will never end.

Don't Think You're the Only One
Morgan Lanza
Walter Hill Elementary School, Grade 3

      I love the story that my Mom tells me about when I came home from Kentucky in my Mom's arms. I was adopted, and that makes me special. I had just been born. My parents came to see me in the middle of the night. They got to hold me right away.
      My birth Mom got to hold me, too. Just because my birth Mom gave me up doesn't mean that she didn't love me. She just wanted me to have a happy, better life. She didn't think she could spend the time with me that she wanted to.
      So all the people in the world that are adopted.... don't think you are the only one adopted. Because you're not. I really, really love my parents – both the ones that gave me up and the ones that I live with now.

Step by Step
Chasity Johnson
Thurman Francis Arts Academy, Grade 6

Step by step, day by day
These are the things that get me through:
The precious feeling of a heartbeat;
The acceptance of one breath after another;
Seeing the future in my eyes;
But no matter what happens, I know these things will get me through life.

Why...
Logan Garrett
McFadden School of Excellence, Grade 7

Why do we play?
Why do we lie?
Every single day
I want to know why

Who made me?
Who is she?
When is the game?
When will I die?
What are you?
What am I?
Where are we?

Why...

Appreciating

Elizabeth Henry
Riverdale High School, Grade 9

Have you ever thought about if everything you had was taken way?
What would you do if the roof over your head was stripped from you?
Can you imagine if every piece of food you had was taken from your table?
What would you do if every single thing you worked hard for was gone?

Would you appreciate it then?
Would you appreciate the job you have or the public education you received?
Would you finally understand that everything you complain about was insignificant?

Why is it that we only appreciate things when they are gone?
Why is it we don't show people that we care for them?
What if you lost a loved one and hadn't told them how you felt about them?

I wish I could turn back time to the one I lost and tell him…
I wish everyday I had appreciated you.
The one I carry so much love for.
I'm sorry for not realizing how much you were worth.
Sorry for not telling you how much I cared for you.
I just want you to know wherever you are …
Just how much I appreciate you now.

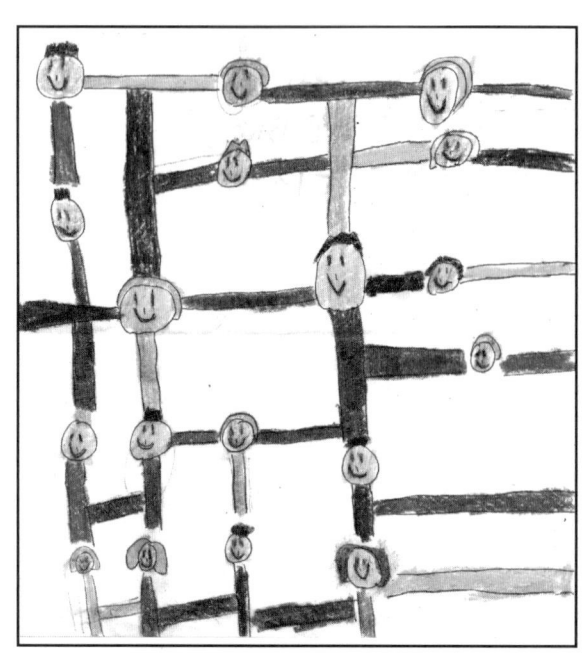

Artwork by Dovie Barrett, Rockvale Elementary School, Grade 4

August 13, Journal (Published Posthumously)
Bruce Gilley
Oakland High School, Grade 9

For the longest time, when asked the question, "Why does God let bad things happen?"...I had no answer...but now I do. Yes, seemingly that would be a great world without sin or evil but when you actually take time to analyze this world you realize how lifeless and emotionless it would be. If we always lived our lives in a constant state of happiness, if there were no ups and downs in life, we would really never be happy at all. Because without evil, there cannot be righteousness; without bad there cannot be good; without ying there cannot be yang; and, most of all, without hate there cannot be love. Think of this so-called perfect world...it would be a world of emotionless machines, because we would always be in one constant state of emotion and nothing would ever change. The main reason God made the world the way it is...is otherwise love would not exist. God made us beings with a choice. If we were all (like I mentioned up there) machines...and had no choice...there would not be real, genuine love. There would just be a feeling we always had only because we had NO OTHER way to feel. Hard to understand I know but try to follow me here. But since God made us have a choice, we know that there are two different paths we can choose. The people who do not accept God for who he is will go down the other. God made two roads because he knew the people that were truly his disciples would choose the one that leads to Him. Ultimately, life comes down to choices and nothing more. We make very common choices everyday that will determine the final outcome of our lives, but then there are the ones that are not so common. The choices not only determine the outcome of our lives, but also define who we are as people - the kind of choices that leaves lasting impacts on people and possibly even the world. Day by day, God gives us His infallible wisdom on how to best handle these life-changing decisions. Now it all comes down to one of those critical choices. Will you listen?

I Hope to Be a Singer
Lainey Edens
Blackman Elementary School, Grade 4

I hope to be a singer with vocal cords so fine,
And hope to have some songs that I can call all mine.
I am going to go on tour and meet some famous people,
Zoe Girl, Jesse McCartney are all fine and cheerful.
Music is a hobby of mine,
It's better than collecting rocks or collecting lime.
I'll wear flashy pants and a snakeskin shirt,
Not some breeches, not some eye glasses, not some skirts.
I will have two limos and live in a mansion,
I will not be held for ransom.
I'll be in the Hall of Fame and sing at a rodeo,
I might even sing on the radio
I know I am just a girl that can sing,
But when you read this poem you will know that I can DREAM.

Autumn
Marisa Jenkins
Roy Waldron School, Grade 4

Autumn is a pretty season
Understanding why we celebrate Thanksgiving
To come outside and jump in the leaves
Under the leaves we look at the sky
Making a big pile under the tree
Nothing but raking leaves.

The People Who Really Count

Abe Stoklasa
Eagleville High School, Grade 12

When there isn't a cloud in the sky
And the time's just passing by
And no one wonders why,
Everyone is there.

When there isn't a worry in the world
And all have danced and twirled
And our perfect side to life unfurled
Everyone is there.

When nothing is going wrong
And all are getting along
And life is a big happy song
Everyone is there.

When things are going great
And no one is full of hate
And there's nothing left to debate
Everyone is there.

But, when push comes to shove
And there's just not enough love
And we see what people are really made of
Only you are there.

And when things get tough
And the world gets rough
And people just don't care enough
Only you are there.

And when people you thought you could trust
Turn their backs to you in utter disgust
And your big chain of love starts to rust
Only you are there.

So when things aren't going your way
And you are just having a bad day
Don't ever look away
Because I will be there.

I Am like a Blizzard

Justin Peery
Blackman Middle School, Grade 7

I am like a blizzard,
All bitter cold inside,
Throwing snowballs,
Making snowmen,
I am like a blizzard.

Life

Katie Leverette
Eagleville High School, Grade 12

As high-spirited kids we think twice about nothing
Digging dirt from the back yard to make mud pies
Knowing the whole time we're chefs
Looking through our beginner's telescopes into the black sky
Awakening the inner astronauts in ourselves.

As high-strung teens we think twice about everything
Digging through our strewn rooms to find last night's homework
Only to find that it's not there
Looking through our entire closets
Dreadfully finding nothing to wear.

As highly ambitious, young adults there's nothing we fail to think about
Digging through piles of college pamphlets and applications
Searching for a strong foothold in the climb toward the future
Looking down each path laid before us
Only time will tell where that path will lead us.

Always Been a Dream for Me
Melissa Vickers
Smyrna Elementary School, Grade 5

I've always had a dream to be a teacher one day.
Standing at the board teaching math, students asking questions, and me answering them has always been a dream for me.
Talking to other teachers during my break time and watching kids play in P.E. has always been a dream for me.
Eating lunch with my class and talking to them, going outside and watching them play on the monkey bars, and coming in and my class smelling like sweat has always been a dream for me.
Then ending the day by going home has always been a dream for me.
I hope to make a difference in their lives one day by helping them fill their dreams of becoming somebody.
I've always had a dream to be a teacher one day.

Karate
Elizabeth Pitts
Smyrna Primary School, Grade 4

Educational, fundamental, punching
Cat stance, Zenkutsu stance, side stance
Kicking, sparring, games
Bend in stances, sweaty, hard-working
Get tips, tired, push-ups
Sit-ups, roundhouse kick, front kick.

I feel connected to the Japanese because I get to learn more about karate!

Oh I Wish I Could Be a Teacher
Nathan Creech
Blackman Elementary School, Grade 3

Oh I wish I could be a teacher,
All the children looking at me.
Oh I wish I could be a teacher,
And then I will have a key.
Oh I wish I could be a teacher,
Sitting in a comfortable seat.
Oh I wish I could be a teacher,
Oh all the people I would meet.
Oh I wish I could be a teacher,
And I'll teach people how to rhyme.
Oh I wish I could be a teacher,
Oh I would have a very fun time.
Oh I wish I could be a teacher,
I would work all day till the end of May.

The Waves
Elizabeth Ingle
Oakland High School, Grade 11

Fright is an ocean
Crashing like waves
Smothering quickly, drowning slowly
In the depths of your mind.

Life Ring
Robert Johnson
Thurman Francis Arts Academy, Grade 6

All life is connected to each and every thing,
And all those little things,
Are connected,
In life's ring.
The ring of life circles around God's hand,
So he can keep the perfect balance,
And all those little things,
Make life's perfect little ring.

Black and White
Anthony Myers
Oakland High School, Grade 10

In the world of black and white,
All you see is day and night.
I have seen this world in my eyes.
It is a place where there are no skies.
Good and evil
Love and hate
What color could you see in this state?
But I found the color in her eyes
Oh, such a magnificent blue.
All I saw was her love,
through and through.
We talked for hours
Of endless nights,
And now we dream on forever
What a colorful sight!

The Fight for America
Robbie Mosley
Thurman Francis Arts Academy, Grade 6

I feel very sad
Something happened that was bad
I dreaded that day
I think the people that planned it should pay
They crashed planes into both towers
I will dread all of those bad hours
I am thankful for the soldiers fighting in Iraq
I hope we don't get another attack
I am glad that the soldiers are fighting for me
I won't forget that they are fighting to keep America free.

My Dream
Wesley Parker
Lascassas Elementary School, Grade 3

     My biggest dream is to some day be a firefighter so I can save peoples' lives. I got my dream from the men that helped people at the Twin Towers on September 11th. Firefighters are very brave men and women. It takes a very special person to do this job. I think I could be that person. This is my dream.

Threads
Sarah Riddle
Oakland High School, Grade 12

Third row from the front
Dead center
Eyes directly ahead
Oblivious to everyone around;
But there is a connection.

Keen eyes are able to see
The tangled web of thread
Different colors intertwine
Shades all around;
But there is a connection.

The darker the color, the deeper the attachment.
Threads reveal our deepest secrets.
These threads of color are attached to all;
So there is always a connection.

Keep These Three
Matthew Taylor
Oakland High School, Grade 11

Sacrifice is given up,
Loyalty is given to,
Honor is given through.
Sacrifice is willingness to die,
Loyalty is standing side by side,
Honor is earned and taken to heart.
All of these are major parts.
Honor, sacrifice, and loyalty, too
Can all be shared through someone like you.
Make sacrifices for your loved ones.
Keep loyalty to the Almighty One.
Gain your honor through the way you live.
And never be too proud to forgive.

When I Grow Up
KaraLynne Levi
Wilson Elementary School, Grade 1

    I want to teach kindergarten when I grow up. I want to be a teacher because I want to help kids. I would ask my kids about their hobbies. Then I would write it down for them. They will be good in class and I will have fun.

Connected?
Baker Colvert
Oakland High School, Grade 12

Phones
Cell phones
Instant messengers and e-mail
Always connected . . .
Or farther apart?

The Fire Department
Justin Stile
Walter Hill Elementary School, Grade 5

    My dad, Chris Stiles, is a captain for the Walter Hill Volunteer Fire Department. When I grow up, I want to become a firefighter just like my dad. I get to go with my dad to some of his meetings and trainings. When I become thirteen years old, I will be able to join as a junior firefighter. The reason I am interested in becoming a firefighter is because I see how much our fire department cares about its community and helping others. It makes me feel good to help others. This is a way that I can give back to my community. Being a firefighter takes a lot of time and training, but it is worth it. Everyone there feels like one big family.

When I Grow Up
Alexa Vale
Blackman Elementary School, Grade 1

When I grow up I whant to be aather and I think it will be fun. I whant to write non ficshan books becas I want to write abote rele things and I want to liven in kintuke and write books there.

Disconnection
Graham Overton
Oakland High School, Grade 12

Hypocrisy runs rampant,
Disconnecting what's true and what's false.
Black and white, what's the difference?
Color, my friend!
Color disconnects!

I Mite Be a Plesman
Nathan Luther
Blackman Elementary School, Grade 1

I mite be a plesman win I gro up. Her is why I want to be a plesman. To save people. I want to put bad geys in jale. Its my thing. I like plesman. I like plesman becose they have handcofs.

Escape the Sounds
Sarah Rademacher
Oakland High School, Grade 10

    The TV soundtrack of many lives is
sometimes my worst enemy. The glass box
craftily catches my eyes, and refuses to let me go.
I behold illusions, the array of colors, and pleasures.
    Characters lead lives far beyond my ordinary
existence. The electronic wonder has the power
to hypnotize me, an innocent viewer.
    But I can choose to refuse to be caught in the
web of fanciful fantasies. I must beware not to get too
close, nor stay too long. For my own thoughts,
lying neglected within will soon die, diffuse,
and I may cease to hear that still, small voice,
the calling sound of silence.

Horses of the Wild
Michelle Moore
Homer Pittard Campus School, Grade 5

        Manes flying through the sky
        Necks reaching for the stars
        Eyes bright as crystal light
        Ears perked till bright daylight
        Muscles stretching for the moon
        Hooves pounding dirt just torn
        Tails waving in the wind
        Minds open to the world
        Spirits running wild.

I Want to be a Vet
Emily Boone
Blackman Elementary School, Grade 1

I want to be a vet cuas I like animls and I want to fix thim. Ther are lots of animls and pets. I like hrosis.

Rain
Sarah Hudson
Homer Pittard Campus School, Grade 5

>Rain makes everything wet
>Drip drop, drip drop
>It's something I've just met
>Drip drop, drip drop.
>
>People bring out umbrellas of size
>Drip drop, drip drop
>Those people are very wise
>Drip drop, drip drop.
>
>It rains in everyday life
>Drip drop, drip drop
>It comes from way up high
>Drip drop, drip drop.
>
>You'll see people running
>Drip drop, drip drop
>And it is so funny
>Drip drop, drip drop.
>
>Everyone pops to shelter
>Drip drop, drip drop
>But suddenly it stops
>Drip...drop...drip...drop.

Sports
Tyler Allen
Wilson Elementary School, Grade 5

Speed
Practice
Outs
Running bases
Trying hard
Stepping up to the plate

Raiders

Taylor Johnson
Siegel High School, Grade 10

      I panted and dragged the 5-gallon water tank as far as I could before it's weight dragged into the mud preventing me from going any farther. "Allen! Take the water tank from Johnson! Johnson, get on the stretcher!" yelled our commander Wade Dunaway at us. I grunted as I relieved Allen of the stretcher.
      "Come on, guys! You have this!" yelled the grader, Taylor Wall, in encouragement. We reached the low crawl. One foot of water, two feet of mud… Yum… We lowered ourselves down. The 100 pound sand bag tied to the stretcher imitating a human body began to slip. I grabbed it and pulled it back on to the stretcher, trying to quickly tighten the straps. We lowered the stretcher onto the ground and began trying to work it through the low crawl, but the metal stirrups caught the mud and began dragging. We were crawling inch by inch... Colonel Chaffin, yelling support from the sidelines screamed, "Lift it!"
      An idea struck me. Okay, we were going nowhere. Everyone was pushing and pulling at the wrong times…. We needed to get our timing right. "Guys! On the count of three, we pull and lift! Ready! One, Two, THREE!" I screamed. The stretcher moved! Not just a half an inch, but like, eight inches! "One, two, THREE! One, two, THREE!" I kept up the rhythm; finally we reached the end of the low crawl. We reached behind us as soon as the stretcher was out, and got the ammunition can, and the water tanks, and the demilitarized weapons. I allowed myself a small smile of pride. Then we were off, running through the muck and mire of Cedars-of-Lebanon Cross Country Rescue Course 2004 Raider Competition. We did a couple more obstacles – an eight-foot wall and a log. We finally made it to the finish line.
      This is just a taste of what the JROTC raider teams do at competitions every year. We also live in the woods for three days, no showers, no electricity. We run two to four miles, do two minutes sit-ups and pushups, obstacle course/decathlon, map reading test, land navigation, and some other events, living off of cardboard-tasting heater meals.
      This is who we are. This is what we do. This is what connects us. When we go back to school, we're just normal kids again, with homework and tests, but at just the right moment, when we look into each other's eyes, we see a gleam of something left over, something inside us that makes us different from all the others…something full of pride and self-acknowledgement.
      We are the Raiders.

My Life
Joshua Greer
Homer Pittard Campus School, Grade 5

My life is like the weather
The weather is like my life
When it's rainy I am sad
Look it's shining
Now I'm glad.

My life is like a book
A book is like my life
When I'm mad my pages are closed
When I'm in a soccer game
My pages are blowing in the wind.

My life is like a box
A box is like my life
When I'm embarrassed I am burned
When I'm steamed I am preserved.

My life is like a candle
A candle is like my life
Always lit up
Never burnt out.

A baby cub is small
Small am I
This is me
And my life.

Listen
Molly Guest
Smyrna High School, Grade 11

Words run wild,
Reckless like the sea
I fade into the background
Will anyone listen to me?

The words were like a song,
Speaking to the heart
Precious and unique
Like a priceless piece of art.

Screaming so loud
Apollo himself can hear
Starting to lose hope
I begin to disappear.

Forgotten and unwanted,
I am pushed down
My every hope demolished
My soul begins to frown.

Words run wild,
Reckless like the sea
I fade into the background
Will anyone listen to me?

Veterans
Meranda Johnson
Wilson Elementary School, Grade 5

Very brave
Earning our freedom
Treat them with respect
Entering danger
Risking their lives for us
Away from home and family
Nation of heroes
Saving our country.

What is Love?
Aimee Albert
Siegel High School, Grade 10

A word to say from sister to brother,
A feeling we have for one another.
A passionate way to show that we care,
Or a need to know that we'll always be there.
Is love really good; is it really all that great?
Is it planned out by others or controlled by fate?
Some say love is blind, and I think that's true
Because love couldn't see how much I loved you.
Love will bring people together and back apart,
Love will overwhelm you and break your heart.
The bad thing about love is it will not hide,
It always shows when you have it inside.
Love was there every time I looked in your eyes,
Love was there when we watched the sun rise.
But in the end was love there for us?
Was love going to be enough?
It wasn't there all the nights you made me cry,
Baby, love wasn't there the day you said goodbye.

If Only...
Anna Potts
Wilson Elementary School, Grade 4

If only there was peace,
If only we'd looked like we want to look,
If only people would treat us like we should be treated,
If only we could live God's way,
If only the war was over,
If only the world was peaceful,
If only the people we love would come home,
If only the animals could live forever,
If only the birds sang louder,
If only the crickets chirped louder,
If only people could live forever,
If only people's feelings mattered to people,
If only people cared about people,
If only all of these things could happen, we could have peace in the world.

The First Day of School
Nicole Warrick
LaVergne Middle School, Grade 7

The first day of school,
Is always very cool.
You do nothing all day,
Except have fun and play.
You don't get your books,
So people worry about looks.
The first day of school,
Is always very cool.

Connections
Tyler Little
Wilson Elementary School, Grade 5

Friends have connections.
Moms and dads have love connections.
So connections are like phone lines
Connected not with cords,
But with friends and family.

Artwork by Macy Swanager, Thurman Francis Arts Academy, Grade 8

I Am Sarah
Sarah Baker
Christiana Elementary School, Grade 5

I am responsible and respectful.
I wonder how many people are on Earth.
I hear animals.
I see a hurt animal and save it.
I want a black bear hamster.
I am responsible and respectful.

I pretend I am a vet.
I feel sad when one of my pets die.
I touch snakes.
I worry about animals.
I cry when I think about my other friends.
I am responsible and respectful.

I understand my punishments.
I say that I will fulfill my dreams.
I dream of becoming a vet.
I try my hardest to do well in school.
I hope I will become a vet.
I am responsible and respectful.

I Am Unique
Asha Phillips
McFadden School of Excellence, Grade 1

I am unique because my mom is pail and my dad is dark brown. I am tan and so is my sister. I like being tan. People say that. I am so pretty and my sister too. We say thank you. So that's how I am unique.

I Want to Be a Falcons Football Player
Alex Edens
Blackman Elementary School, Grade 2

When I grow up, I want to be a Falcons football player. I would smell a lot of stuff like the lockers and the room and the air, too. I would taste the Gatorade in my mouth at half time. I would hear the crowd when I scored. I would hear the loud scoreboard. I would run to score a touchdown when two guys tried to tackle me. Also, I would see the cheerleaders cheering at half time. We would win. Then we'd go out to eat.

Dreams
Taylor Petty
Walter Hill Elementary School, Grade 3

Dreams of singing
Roses so red
Exciting times
Always having fun
Moving forward
Special memories.

Baseball Is Life
Caroline Faulkner
Blackman Elementary School, Grade 2

Bases, bats, and balls – that's what I need for my future. I dream of being a professional female baseball player. I will achieve my dream by working hard. The reason I like baseball is I like the coaches, getting dirty, and just being a part of the team.

CONNECTIONS
Mrs. Reta Barney's Class
Smyrna Primary School, Grade 2

C is for confidence
O is for openness
N is for neighbors who live next door
N is for nice – a great way to be
E is for everyone who encourages me
C is for courage to love my enemies
T is for truth that sets me free
I is for inquisitive children to learn more
O is for opportunity that learning gives me to succeed
N is for the National Guard who defends my country
S is for satisfaction for a job well done.

Back Porch Poet

Brittney Benton
Smyrna West Alternative School, Grade 12

Lying awake at night
No sleep in my ways,
I know I'm getting restless
Haven't made my bed in days.
So let this back porch poet
Sing your precious soul to sleep,
Maybe I'll find comfort
Instead of a reason to weep.
Imagining that you're here
Instead of always gone,
How is it so easy
To break an unbreakable bond?
I miss you like crazy
And will until you're here,
I will keep on crying
Til' you're here to catch my tears.
So let this back porch poet
Sing your precious soul to sleep,
Maybe I'll find comfort
Instead of a reason to weep.

How Long?
Angela Rudd
Riverdale High School, Grade 12

The walls are closing
My life's running thin
How long can I carry
This life full of sin.

Lies, hates
Cheats, and steals
These are the things
One does and feels.

The perfect people
are never around
never been seen
and are not to be found.

How much longer
Can I take this
Living the life
Of a treacherous bliss.

Not for long
I beg and plead
Find me a place
With no misery.

A Friend's Vow

Amber Stine
Christiana Middle School, Grade 8

How can anybody really know?
What kind of bond we share
And even if I told them
Who would really care?

You are very dear to me
I hope you know it's true
And now that you are moving away
What am I to do?

And when you are gone
A part of me will be lost
I feel I have taken our friendship for granted
And now I'm paying the cost.

I never knew how much you meant to me
Until you went away
The thought of you being far away
Haunts me everyday.

And now I make this vow to you
To keep until the end
I'll help you through this move
And be here through thick and thin.

So if you ever need a friend
You know just whom to call
I'll be here by the phone
In case you need anything at all.

Tears

Thomas Patton
LaVergne Middle School, Grade 8

It was the time of terror,
It was the year of fear,
Ever since the attack of terror,
We have been in tears.

Loved ones were lost,
Friends disappeared,
Ever since the towers fell,
The world has been in tears.

If you do not know anyone that was lost,
Think about how others feel,
Ever since 9/11,
Everyone has been in tears.

Nobody moved,
They stopped all time,
Ever since Lady Liberty cried,
America has been in tears.

Ever since that fateful day,
I have had many fears,
But when I think back to 9/11,
I am in tears.

They say that time heals all wounds,
But this wound cannot be healed,
For this wound leaves a scar,
And time, will forever, be in tears.

Puzzle Pieces
Taylor Ezell
Christiana Middle School, Grade 8

Sometimes I think about life
I think about my future
I think about you…
I think about how our hands fit
Like a puzzle
You know,
The million-piece kind
And you're
The last
Piece
Knowing I have that kind of connection…
With someone
Like
You.

Food Fight
Katie Williams
Buchanan Elementary School, Grade 6

Food fight
Yells a kid
Slash
Bong
Clop
You hear the battle around you
Pinnggg
Goes a girl's lunch money on the floor
Chu-ching
The cash register goes
Whir
Of a principal's whistle
And its silence.

The School Year
Kevin Havard
David Youree Elementary School, Grade 5

August

Fresh, new

Beginning, learning, studying

Books, homework, tests, dances

Ending, exciting

Vacation, freedom

June

Lawyer
Spencer Ford
Central Middle School, Grade 8

Though I know not your trouble yet,
You I shall not soon forget,
'Cause no matter how the future goes,
You came to me, my sal'ry rose.

In an accident? Oh my!
With your fee, a car I'll buy.
I'll win the case, but if we lose,
A brand new 'vet I still will choose.

Need a defense? Just come to me!
And at my office I will be,
You will not go to jail just yet,
That is, if you can pay your debt.

Memorized, I've every law,
Just tell me what the witness saw,
And I will make a case for you,
For more than just a buck or two.

Loved Ones
Katie Miller
David Youree Elementary School, Grade 5

A soldier walks home.

Everyone will remember.

The day that peace came.

They celebrated.

They cried with joy in their eyes.

It was all over.

People remembered.

A Dream
Ethan Floyd
Blackman Elementary School, Grade 2

I have a dream to live on a beach, because I like the sounds of the great waves. I also like the feeling of the wet ocean on my hands and the sounds of happy young children. I hope that dream happens one day.

Day
Rebecca Carden
David Youree Elementary School, Grade 5

Days, days like a maze,

Crazy, lazy kinds of days.

Days, days sometimes loud,

Sometimes proud, sometimes mad, sometimes very, very bad.

But hopefully lots of very, very glad days.

Butterfly Dance
Mrs. Sunita Watson's Class
Barfield Elementary School, Grade 2

Gentle, lovely, lonely
Fragile, pretty
Bringing happiness.

Flying together
Flying high, flying low
Flying fast, flying slow
Flying above the ocean
Flying free.

Colorful, terrific
Dancing in joy
Dancing in peace
Sweet butterfly garden
Fly gracefully
Fly in peace.

Artwork by Krystin Massa, Thurman Francis Arts Academy, Grade 6

Peer Mentoring

Rachel La Forte
Smyrna High School, Grade 12

Outnumbered
By inexperience and optimism,
In a room with
Youth and naïveté,
Almost as if a
Generation separates us.
All that I was,
That I remember so
Tenderly,
Is all that they are,
But don't even realize.
Unsuspecting,
They will be
Tested,
Tormented, and
Tempted,
But it is my fervent hope
That they will
Surmount their
Unyielding legacy,
And become all
That I believe
I am.

The Connection

Jessica Wright
Christiana Middle School, Grade 8

I pick up my flute and begin to play
As I play
I see people from the past.
There are soldiers going off to war
A couple beginning their life together
A congregation singing praises
Children singing and playing together
Wives humming as they fold clothes
Past, present, future
It connects us all.
Music.

DO MORE
Ronise Ephord
Smyrna High School, Grade 12

DO MORE THAN EXIST
LIVE

DO MORE THAN LOOK
OBSERVE

DO MORE THAN HEAR
LISTEN

DO MORE THAN LISTEN
UNDERSTAND

DO MORE THAN THINK
PONDER

DO MORE THAN TALK
SPEAK THE TRUTH

DO MORE THAN READ
ABSORB

DO MORE THAN TOUCH
FEEL

DO MORE THAN CARE
LOVE.

Dark
Austin Poteete
Blackman Middle School, Grade 6

    Darkness, it's all around, and I can't believe that it's everywhere I am. I used to be happy, but no more. I feel angry at the world. My mom is my only comfort and sometimes she doesn't even comfort me. I feel sad because no one cares. I feel alone!
    Anger overwhelms me like a monster living inside me, and no one cares. Ever since my dad died three years ago, I've felt this way. But no one listens, no one cares. Then, my mom comes home, and I feel happy. It's almost like the monster in the dark corners of my heart disappears.

I Am

Kate Simpson
Thurman Francis Arts Academy, Grade 5

I am—I am strong, unique, awesome, me.
I wonder how the future will roll out into my palms.
I hear—I hear the sounds of the leaves when they hit the ground and how they float in
     the wind.
I see—well, I see a seed on its way to blooming into the rose that it is.
I want to see my family grow to be together and always stand proud.
I am—I am strong, unique, awesome, me.

I pretend that hate is only in a different world and peace will live on.
I believe—I believe that God will find the love in all our hearts . . . forever.
I touch—I touch hearts with this poem, but most of all I touch my own heart.
I feel great, strong, the power of succeeding for the rest of my days.
I worry—I worry sometimes when it is dark if the sun will shine again.
I cry when I hear the sound of my new sister arriving into our world... and I
     welcome her.
I am—I am strong, unique, awesome, me.

I say—I say that God is the best support you will ever have.
I dream to stand on that stage and perform and sing my heart out.
I hope—I hope to live the life I hoped.
I am—I am strong, unique, awesome, ME!

What If
Rachel La Forte
Smyrna High School, Grade 12

An isolated thought
In a schizophrenic
Mind.
The what if's,
Who did's,
How come's,
All grappling for recognition.
But the only idea
I seem to comprehend
In this precious moment,
Is the fact that my shoe is untied,
My make-up is smudged,
And I smell like the work I loathe so.
The only idea you seem to comprehend
In this fleeting moment,
Is the reality that you're running out of gas,
Your essay is a day late,
And, without the slightest hesitation,
You would be okay if this was the first day of
Forever.

Scrambled Dreams
Jessie McMahon
Thurman Francis Arts Academy, Grade 5

Have you ever noticed how,
When you're sleeping your dreams turn upside down?
Your father has the measles,
Though he's had them before,
And a whole new generation comes,
When you open your bedroom door!

Dreams can be of everything,
And anything at all,
They can be humongous,
Big,
Or very, very small!

Nature

Gina Harris
Smyrna High School, Grade 12

This poem is about Mother Nature. Nature, to me, is pure and peaceful, and I want to be like that, and I want the world to be that way also. The poem opens with a description of the beauty of nature, comparing its perfection to society's hate and violence. The end is about how I plan to grow and practice nature's kindness, helping spread her peace.

Her beauty was so obvious
Not a touch of makeup. . .
With the best skin and most delicate smile.
Her hair was all natural,
She had the most amazing figure, with perfect curves.

Her soul was singing,
The melody was angelic. . .
It danced in the wind;
It was like a gypsy
But with a touch of nature.

I want to be her,
But all I can do is stare. . .
I want to share thoughts,
Know and learn from her,
But it wasn't meant, yet.

I'll stand by though,
Remaining from a distance,
Watching. . .learning. . .
And practice feeling her freedom
So I can spread her energy.

And I'll learn her song;
Sing it everywhere I go,
Dancing like her soul.
And perhaps then,
Is when I'll learn of her majestic peace.

Imagination
Sarah Farris
Thurman Francis Arts Academy, Grade 4

I dream, I wonder, I make believe
And someday my imagination will leave
But as for now it's still here and should be for another year.

Do You Ever?
Keela Fults
Lascassas Elementary School, Grade 5

Do you ever think of me and wonder how I am or am I
Just an imprint left in the sand? Do you ever get lonely and
Wish it were I, or are you happy with her, just as
Happy as can be? When you drive by, do you look down my
Road, or are you happy to have her in the passenger seat
To hold? Do you ever grab your pillow and cry unbearable
Tears, or am I the only one that is wishing you were here?

This World of Ours
Danielle Aroujo
Oakland High School, Grade 9

I am a friend
You are an enemy
We are only people
We do what we can.

I see the heavens above
You see the worlds below
We see each other
We meet in the middle.

I feel happy
You feel sad
We all have feelings
We can find our own way.

Two different people
Come together in peace
Together – alone
Can we survive this world of ours?

Today
Hannah Creasey
Lascassas Elementary School, Grade 5

The book just sits here in my lap
As my pencil goes tap, tap, tap.
I look out the window and what do I say,
"Hannah, what are you going to do today?"

The Dreamer
Deborah Anderson
Oakland High School, Grade 9

A locked up box
A broken home
Nothing left to call my own.
A dream, a day
My wish to soar
Barging through a broken door.
I'll dream once more;
I'll wish to fly
With my head always lifted to the sky.

The Best Angel
Matthew Goodman
Oakland High School, Grade 9

When God calls our friends
To dwell with Him up above
We sometimes question him
Where is your love?
Though we can't understand
Why he took our loved ones
We know they are in heaven
Having so much fun.
They made our lives seem easier
And they had no problems
With the words <u>help</u> and <u>give.</u>
God knows how much we need them
So He takes just a few
To make the land of Heaven more beautiful to view.
So when someone we love leaves us
Those of us left behind
Must realize that God chose them
Finding the best angels takes time.

Connecting
Katie Gardner
Christiana Middle School, Grade 7

Connecting, signing in……..
I don't know where I'm going,
But I know
Where I have been.

The process is so slow.
I wait for ten minutes,
But it just won't go.
So I wait a little longer.

I sit here thinking in my head
About where I should go.
I hate not being led,
Though soon I will know.

Eventually it loads,
And I'm ready to go.
This whole process represents the many roads,
But I will be connecting soon, I know.

Artwork by Cristina Brito, Riverdale High School, Grade 12

3:43

Elizabeth Hooper
Oakland High School, Grade 9

I met a stranger one day
Not knowing who he was, I asked
Sir, do you know the time?
Seeing that I was in a hurry, he responded
I am not sure, but let me see.
I waited patiently as he searched for his watch
And I waited
And I waited
Sir, could you please hurry!
The feeble old man turned and these words he spoke
Words I shall never forget.
Why do you hurry around young child?
You are caught in the hustle and bustle of life.
Don't you know that only leads to stress and wrinkles?
I used to be like you, caught up in the ways of the world
Never having time to spend with my wife or son.
Well, my son got older, and my love grew colder.
Oh, sir, I am so sorry; I had no clue. Please forgive me.
Hush child he said. Just listen.
Spend every day as if it is your last.
Sing even if there is no song.
Love when there seems to be no reason.
And then he left, never knowing what those few words meant to me.
Oh, yeah, he called back, it's 3:43.

Autumn
Jordan Mingis
Cedar Grove Elementary School, Grade 4

It feels like autumn.
Leaves in my hair,
Rake in my hand,
Jacket is on,
I feel autumn in the air.

I see autumn in the air.
Leaves falling everywhere,
Sky so blue,
Jack- o-lanterns so bright,
I see autumn everywhere.

I hear autumn everywhere.
Water running sweetly,
Leaves crunching soundly,
Bird tweeting loudly.
I hear autumn in the air.

I can taste autumn everywhere.
Pumpkin pie,
Turkey and apple cider,
Candy so sweet,
I am tasting things in autumn.

Where People Can Connect
Ella Strawman
Oakland High School, Grade 9

Corporations
Organizations
Nations
Networks
Enterprises
Clubs
Teams

Fall Is in the Air

Tyler Brooks
Cedar Grove Elementary School, Grade 4

It feels like autumn…
Crunchy leaves in my hand,
Morning mist in my land,
Northern winds ruffle my hair,
Bringing in sweet, cool air.

It looks like autumn…
Leaves are a colored friend,
Dancing with a whirlwind,
Squash of bright yellow,
Pumpkins are a scary fellow.

It sounds like autumn…
Leaves rattle in the trees,
Then fall softly and silently,
Children snickering pranks,
Families gathering, saying thanks.

It tastes like autumn…
Gobble, gobble no more,
Turkey behind the oven door,
Granny brought something sweet
Warm pumpkin pie for me to eat.

Chains

Carly Davis
McFadden School of Excellence, Grade 6

These chains bind us together,
They link the threads of time.
They are everywhere, here forever,
Connecting every line.

The weakest chains are tiny and thin,
They are relationships that break and bend.
The strongest come from inside,
The binding ones, we rarely hide.

Even the strongest chains sometimes break.
They leave our hearts to ache and ache.
These chains have no limitations or rules,
They can spring from nowhere and shimmer like jewels.

These chains bind us together,
They link the threads of time
They are everywhere, here forever,
Connecting every line.

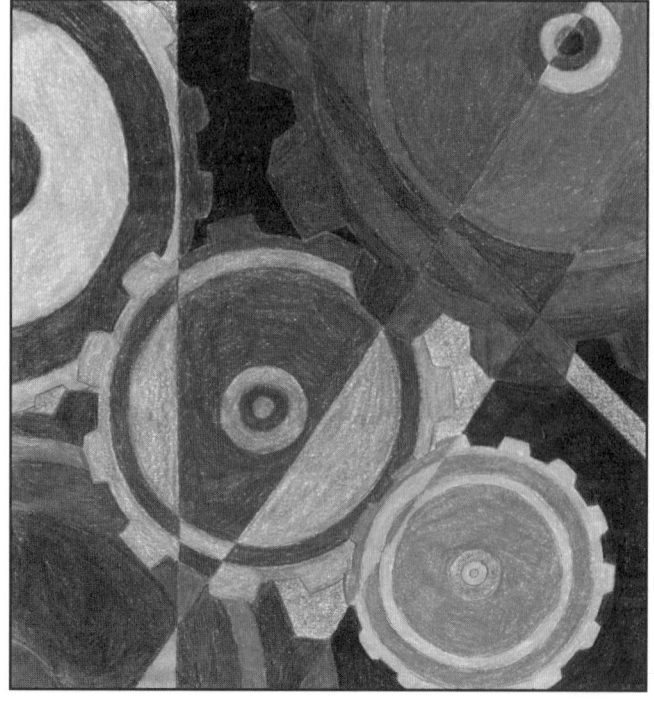

Artwork by Brady Seymore, Siegel High School, Grade 12

Chapter Three

Connecting through Fond Memories

I Remember
Skyler Holder
Siegel High School, Grade 9

I remember the wind blowing that night.
I remember the sky being dark and cloudless.
I remember a big yellow moon.
What happened to that wonderful peace?
I remember a deep rumble in the distance.
I remember clouds forming overhead.
I remember the moon disappearing.
I remember the wind picking up.
I remember a terrible howling noise.
I remember hail falling from the sky.
I remember raindrops pounding on the roof.
I remember riding in a car.
I remember being very little.
I remember that was my first storm.

First Football Game
Mathew Bohannon
David Youree Elementary School, Grade 5

Wake up in the morning, its game day.
Time to get dressed and ready to play.
Out on the field, don't know what to do.
Then I knew what to do.
You hit him high and you hit him low.
Down, set, hike, off we go.

I Remember
Sonny Yang
Rock Springs Middle School, Grade 7

I remember the dark cold draft of wind as we crossed street to street.
I remember the light smiles as the door opened.
I remember my bag being filled at each house with those light faces smiling at me.
I remember a light, warm smile and hug waiting for me.
I remember Halloween.

Christmas
Caitlin Cheadle
Christiana Middle School, Grade 8

Smelling the sweet aroma of orange and cinnamon
Watching the clouds form a snowman
Riding along in a horse-drawn buggy
Tasting bitter sweet honey.

Giving and receiving
Pleasing and believing.

Watching smiles light up the world
Drinking eggnog by a candlelit dinner
Visiting Grams and Gramps
Everything is so perfect.

It's Christmas!

Memories
Danielle Vincion
Rockvale Elementary School, Grade 8

The memories with friends
The times we shared
The laughs we laughed
The mistakes we made
The trouble we caused
The people we met and the people we loved
The hopes and dreams we had
The life we were going to share together
Then, someone else comes along, you drift apart
Because of silly little things
Then you never talk
You walk past one another like a stranger
When the truth is, you don't know anyone better
Then your life flies by, never speaking again
And you always think to yourself, "Were we ever really even friends?"
The memories will always stand.

Victory
Jessica Blankenship
Christiana Middle School, Grade 8

Time is running out
We're losing by one point
I get the ball
The pressure is on
Adrenaline is rushing while I am lost and unsure
People on my left; people on my right
I go for it
I run; the crowd goes wild
I stop, jump, and take the shot…
Everyone runs to the court where I stand speechless
It hits me then
I just scored the winning basket
Happiness takes place.

The Buzzer Beater
Peyton Motroni
Blackman Elementary School, Grade 3

It was the game of the week,
And everyone was there.
The "Heat" was playing,
And the other team didn't prepare.

Passes were thrown,
And shots were made.
The score was tied.
The minutes started to fade.

My feet were on the 3-point line,
And my heart was pounding.
The ball went into the air,
And the buzzer was sounding.

As the ball made a swish,
And went through the net,
This will be the game
I will never forget!

My Favorite Memory
Dakota Smith
Smyrna Primary School, Grade 1

We went camping at the campgrounds and we made smores. We went fishing at the lake and I caught a catfish. Me and my dad cooked and ate it.

A Raggedy Ann
Allison Anderson
Wilson Elementary School, Grade 1

Last summer, I played softball on the Raggedy Anns. Once, when I was up to bat, the coach pitched the ball and I hit the ball over the first baseman's head. I kept running and running until I came to home base. I was so tired and really happy. I had made a homerun! We also won the game.

My Favorite Memory
Desirae Parrish
Smyrna Primary School, Grade 1

At Easter, I found an Easter egg on a gate. A parent had to help me get it down. When I got it, it had an M&M pack in it and the M&M's were very, very good. I hope I'll get as much as I did last time.

Homeroom King
Parker Burgess
Thurman Francis Arts Academy, Grade 6

>Imagine me, Parker
>Breaking the world record for home runs.
>Hours, days, and weeks of practice.
>Imagine me, running the bases to get to home plate.
>I'm almost there,
>Feeling the rush of the crowd,
>Screaming my name.
>I touch home plate,
>And the crowd roars.
>Wow!
>This is awesome!

My Favorite Memories
Paige Gronbach
Smyrna Primary School, Grade 1

I helped my mommy make meatballs for supper. I helped my daddy wash the car. I helped my brother do his homework for his teacher. He helps me do my homework for my teacher. On Halloween, I scared all the kids. I help other kids. At our fall fun day we had fun.

Movie Memory
Tanner Nokes
Thurman Francis Arts Academy, Grade 6

I'll tell you something grand about one day I had
My mom and I had a special day
That made me feel what words can't say
We loaded up and off we went
A day together to be spent
So many choices. What would we do?
I thought of a movie for just us two
The latest spy movie was Cody Banks
So we bought buttered popcorn and two large drinks
Picking our seats, we decided on the middle
Then I decided I needed some Skittles
The action and the adventure made me daydream I was him
I'd wear a black suit when I was not in the gym
After it was over, we went back home
I enjoyed our day out and took off the phone
I called my friend Zeben, told him it was real cool
Then I had to go to bed because the next day was school.

My Football Game
Dejuan Martin
Smyrna Primary School, Grade 2

    I hear my coach blow the whistle when it's time to stop. The football drops and we huddle and try not to crumble or fumble. I lead my team to victory not misery, but it's not all about me. See, this football game is team sport and it takes everyone to help me score! I like working hard to be number 22.

One December Morning
Tristan Rush
Blackman Elementary School, Grade 5

It was a cold December morning and I had just woke up from a good night of rest. I jumped out of bed and realized it was Christmas. I rushed downstairs and there was the Christmas tree and under it were tons of presents. I knew then that it was going to be a special morning.

I had a lot of presents under the tree for me. I got a laser tag set, a racecar, and a pair of skates. My parents were sitting on the couch watching me open my presents. All of a sudden they handed me a package. I opened the package and inside of it was a puppy! It was a Labrador Retriever. It was the cutest puppy I had ever seen. This was the best Christmas ever!

After Christmas the puppy grew and grew. It got stronger and faster. I had to give him a bath or two but he was still fun. I love that puppy very much. He is my best friend and is there for me whenever I need a friend. The Christmas I got him for a present was the most special moment I ever had.

Artwork by Danielle Burr, Cedar Grove Elementary School, Grade 5

Memories

Tucker Webb
LaVergne Middle School, Grade 7

I have a lot of memories,
some that might be lost;
memories of snow,
when windshields turned to frost.

Memories of family
that may have passed away;
or gathering school supplies
at the end of the school day.

Memories of friends,
new, but mostly old;
putting on Dad's suit jacket,
whenever I was cold.

Memories of Hot Wheels,
whenever I was young;
doing mean things to my sister
like sticking out my tongue.

Memories of walking,
out in a fog;
dreaming that someday,
I could get a dog.

Memories are good,
no matter what people say;
I have a lot of memories,
and I hope that they can stay.

James Island, South Carolina
Jacob Richardson
McFadden School of Excellence, Grade 8

In South Carolina,
there's a place called James Island
where my heart and soul truly lie.
I can always feel the winds from the Atlantic calling me,
smell crab cakes cooking in the kitchen,
hear laughter and birds,
see the marshes and the Charleston skyline.

I remember good times and bad times,
those great days and nights,
and an occasional splinter.

Then I feel myself racing in the wind.
Through the harbor we go
as we dodge boats and buoys alike.
When a great tanker enters the bay,
the wake brings us up and down, over and over.

And then we begin our return
to Anne and Dave's James Island home.

Cookie Day
Shannon Aderholt
Blackman Elementary School, Grade 3

My Grammy, Aunt Cindy, Mom, and I all bake Christmas cookies on the Saturday after Thanksgiving. We bake around twenty different recipes from scratch. We end up with thousands of cookies. We use a lot of sugar and flour. We always have fun. It has been a family tradition for many years. We enjoy sharing our cookies with many people. I look forward to it every year.

My Grandfather's Words
Phillip Dodd
McFadden School of Excellence, Grade 7

I remember the houses and farms, oh so many,
Pop was a sharecropper, so we had to save every penny.

I had three brothers but the cancer took Thurman,
and some friends went to heaven 'cause polio was rampant.

I remember the fire that burned through the roof,
and the hours of labor from six years of age.

I remember the holidays, July 4th and Christmas,
Especially Thanksgiving; the food was delicious.

I remember the parties down by the river;
it was dammed and flooded and is now a lake with a hill in the center.

I see that old Chevy that embarrassed me dearly,
but I'd give anything now just to have it again.

I can still see ol' Shep running away from the river
and saving Mama from the bull that almost hit her.

By putting my ear to the water in the valley,
I could hear all the singing from the church up the river.

I still hear the ridicule and teasing from school;
I only had boots while the others had more.

I hit that home-run and earned instant respect.
My classmates then liked me; no more trouble did I get.

I went to Central when it was a high school
and played in the first football game ever to be held there.

I always felt better when the doctor came
and knew I wanted to do the same.

I remember your grandma, a nurse I ran into;
it was love at first sight, then marriage after med school.

Tumbling down the Stairs
Daniel Warren
Blackman Elementary School, Grade 5

A couple of years ago I arrived at my grandparents' house for Christmas. Now it was December 24, 2001. My grandma whispered in my ear, telling me to be Santa Claus. "NO!" I screamed. "Come on, Daniel." "Ok, fine," I said.

That night nobody knew I was going to be Santa Claus the next morning so I went to my grandparents' room and tried on the suit. "It's a little big," I said to my grandma. "But I'll still wear it."

That night we had our Christmas Eve feast. We had corn, pie, mashed potatoes, baked potatoes, gravy, steamed broccoli, rice, fried shrimp, chicken, and a small turkey. I fell asleep on the couch thinking about what was going to happen the next morning.

The next morning I woke up in my grandparents' room. "Hey, you're awake," my grandma said. "It's five in the morning," I said. "Put this on," she said. When I put it on she said, "Looks great."

When I walked down the stairs I saw my family. The boots were too big so they fell off, and I tumbled down the stairs. They all laughed, and it was the funniest Christmas I ever had.

Connection Rejection
Kalen Johnson
McFadden School of Excellence, Grade 7

She looked at him
He looked away.
She approached him
He ran.
She said, "I like you, Billy."
He screamed, "No!"
She asked, "Why don't you like me?"
He answered, "Duh! Girls have cooties."
She cried, "No, you're wrong."
He said, "No, I'm never wrong."

In a few years…

He looked at her
She looked away.
He approached her
She walked.
He inquired, "Will you go out with me?"
She answered, "You wish."
He asked, "Why not?"
She smirked, "Girls have cooties…remember?"

Memories of Childhood
Sarah Schott
Eagleville High School, Grade 11

Happily skipping, holding my hand

Side by side, playing in the sand

Careless children climbing in trees

Falling down, scraping their knees

Selfish thoughts of ice cream cones

Crying over broken bones

Memories of childhood.

Connections
Mikayla Mityok
Smyrna Elementary School, Grade 2

Once I had to give my cat away, and it made me very sad. We had to give her away because we were moving. I really missed her. She was my very first cat. She was special to me. I learned that letting go of something you love is very hard.

Snow Day
Kayla Goyette
Blackman Middle School, Grade 8

Under the covers,
Too warm to move,
Wanting to stay in bed,
'Til late afternoon.
Little did I know,
When I just wanted to sleep,
A winter adventure waited for me.
As the sound of excitement opened my eyes,
I opened my window,
But it was caked with ice.
I managed to pull myself out of bed,
And I pushed myself to the window.
I gently slid my hand across to get a clearer look,
And on the ground lay a peaceful blanket of snow.
After a smile spread across my glowing face,
I rushed down the stairs at a very fast pace.
I put on my clothes, and
Then rushed out the door,
The falling snow made the outside a winter wonderland galore.
I'll never forget that day
When I was five years old.
It was my first snow day,
And might I add,
Very cold.

Sweet, Sweet Memories
Victoria Torres
Smyrna Primary School, Grade 5

The sweet, sweet memories I have in my mind
Are the ones that make her so kind.
I love the way we always talked,
And the way we kept our secrets locked.
It was third grade when we first met,
And our friendship will never end, I bet.

Walt Disney World
Bethany
Blackman Elementary School, Grade 3

World excitement
Awesome
Laughing genius
The huge castle
Donald Duck
Ice Cream
Sunshine
Nauseous rides
Extra cotton candy
Yelling
Wonderful
Outstanding
Relaxing vacation
Loved it
Disney is great!

I Had My Birthday Party
Nash Vinkler
Smyrna Primary School, Grade 1

I was happy because I had my birthday. I am happy! I am happy because I had my friends and my Nana and my Mommy.

Memories
Emily Wood
Thurman Francis Arts Academy, Grade 6

Memories are things that people cherish
They stay hidden inside the heart
They help us remember those that perished
And keep us together when we are apart

Memories are things you will never forget
They are ways to show how much you care
For as long as you have memories
Your loved ones will always be there.

Friday Nights!
Sam Douglas
McFadden School of Excellence, Grade 4

Friday nights are always the best.
We hang around and play like it's a fest.
Our parents always do their thing,
Until the phone starts to ring.
The kids play dodgeball,
Even with a football.
It always seems we have a blast,
The time goes by way too fast.
Friday nights are such a treat,
Friends and family are hard to beat.

Thanksgiving
Damien Alcorn
Walter Hill Elementary School, Grade 1

On Thanksgiving, we bowl for the turkey. We eat our turkey. We always talk all the time. We spend time together. We are family.

My Trip To Destin
Tommi Abernathy
Blackman Elementary School, Grade 1

I wint swimming in the pool. I saw a dofin jopeing owt ov the water. I saw a stig ray. I bilt a big sand casul. I sat in the sand. I saw pom tree. I wint to a restrant. I saw segls.

Thanksgiving
Cody Blankenship
Eagleville School, Grade 5

I remember the smell of the turkey and dressing at Thanksgiving dinner.
I remember my family eating and exchanging thoughts.
I remember the pies, casseroles, and sweet potatoes, too, with marshmallows and brown sugar for that sweet taste.
I remember my little cousins, too, with the TV on and the music playing.
I remember my grandmother pulling out cookies after dinner.
I remember Thanksgiving, oh what a joy!
I remember it well, Thanksgiving at Grandma's.

Thanksgiving
Audrey McAteer
Walter Hill Elementary School, Grade 1

On Thanksgiving, I play games. I eat macaroni and cheese. I eat turkey and mashed potatoes. We watch football. We are with our family. Thanksgiving is a holiday. We love our family. We eat green beans.

My Trip to the Beach
Sidney Baker
Blackman Elementary School, Grade 1

 I went to the beach. It was very hot.
 I went in the pool. I had fun.
 My mom jumped in the pool with me.
 It was fun. I had a fun time.

Bluebird
Kaley Stroup
Homer Pittard Campus School, Grade 5

I looked out my window and what did I see? A beautiful bluebird looking back at me. Oh, bluebird why are you still here? Winter's so close and cold weather is near. So fly little bluebird, spread your wings and take flight. Set off from your perch into the cool autumn night. When you wake in the morning to the warmth of the sun, remember we'll meet again when winter is done.

Picture of Hope
Sophie Boehm
Siegel High School, Grade 10

In the dead of night, when velvety darkness encompasses all
A torn photograph, yellowed with age, falls gently,
Landing quietly on a mahogany floor,
Whose dark beams have never before felt the soft touch of footsteps.
The desolate wood gleams in a silver light that cannot be outshined,
And for a glimpse of time, undefined by logical means, life freezes.
Yet Rosa reaches out, defying all laws,
Her long, delicate fingers blindly grasp the tattered snapshot.
What was lost long ago has now been reclaimed.

Going to the Zoo
Nicholas Mazzella
Blackman Elementary School, Grade 1

I see the snakes. The leon was roing. I saw a wale. It sprad water on me. The tiger was fun. I got to pet it.

Melissa
Rachel Rounion
Siegel High School, Grade 10

It was a summer night a few years ago. I can't remember what I was dreaming about. I don't think it was very important. All I know is that I woke up to the sight of a sobbing, frail creature bent over me.

"Rachel, can we talk?" it whispered through tears.

"Of course we can." I immediately opened my arms to invite the tin, yet barely younger body of my sister to lie in my bed. I wiped her tears and traced the strands of her hair gently with the tips of my fingers.

"What will happen when I die?" The question brought to my mind her innocence and how I would give anything to protect that trait in her.

I didn't answer for a while. I lay there and thought about how precious the person in my arms was. Through my whole life I've never had anyone I could trust like I could her. At times she and I have had nothing in the world but each other, but as long as we knew we had at least that, we knew we'd be okay.

In a sort of dream, I began to play our history in my head: giggling, wrestling, crying, and fighting. I remember Christmas at my Grandma's and Thanksgiving at my Aunt's. There was vacation in Florida and visiting family in Michigan. Then there was also listening to my parents fight from the top of the stairs and the divorce papers that were signed a few months afterward. There were the marriages we witnessed between parents and stepparents, and then the marriages we witnessed fail. There were secrets, lies, and there was anger, even hatred. Yet through it all, she and I have remained true to each other. We've been our only constant.

As I remembered the reason that I began thinking this in the first place, I knew how I could answer her question. I laid my head on hers and said very gently, "When you die, I'll be waiting for you so that we can go to Heaven together. I'll be waiting for you because there's no way that there could ever be Heaven for me unless you're there."

She paused a second and said, "You'll be there?"

"Of course I will. I could never go anywhere without you." I began to feel a choking in my throat and the tears well up in my eyes.

"Okay, then, I won't be scared anymore."

At that moment I knew that she would always have her innocence and that everything would be okay. I pulled her closer and neither of us said another word. I remember the dream I had after that well. My little sister and I were toddlers laughing and swinging on a playground. It was dusk, but I wasn't worried, because I knew we would never have to go home.

On the Beach
Kelsey Young
Wilson Elementary School, Grade 4

Sometimes, I remember my first trip to the beach. It was when I was eight years old and I went to New Smyrna Beach with my grandmother. I remember that I could see the beautiful horizon and the waves that were so slowly rising to two feet tall. It was quiet and I can just feel the feeling of that day with my grandmother. We lay on the grainy, brown sand and talked. That afternoon, she put sand all over me and I looked like a mermaid! That night we still stayed and talked until 8:30. My grandmother fell asleep and I had to wake her up. After that, we went back to the hotel and went to sleep. I had not spent time with her in a long time and our time at the beach meant so much to me.

A Fun Beach Trip
Jazmin Scheitel
Blackman Elementary School, Grade 1

Win I wint to the bech me and my cussin digid a holl. We put wattr in the holl and win my little breather wint to the watr prak he road a dollfin. I did it to but oll three uv us wint fast on a wattr slide. My mom and dad wint too. I wint two times. I love it!

I Remember
Karl Luboniecki
Siegel High School, Grade 9

I remember snowy winters,
With snowballs flying every which way

I remember Orlando, Florida,
With a Star Wars thrill ride in the Death Star trench

I remember blazing summers,
Swimming in the pool in our backyard to cool down

I remember seeing the Atlantic,
In my uncle's little fishing boat

I remember Boxwell Scout Camp,
And getting bit by ticks

I remember camping at Cedars of Lebanon,
And finding a nice, quiet spot to think

I remember my first trip to Gatlinburg,
And my ride in the gondola

I remember my first Yom Kippur fast,
And the taste of koogle when we broke fast

I remember always my girlfriend,
And how much I care for her

I remember Mr. Bjork,
And his wonderful sense of humor

I remember my best friend,
And how long I've known him

I remember Christ,
And the sacrifice He made

I remember my place,
So I don't speak out of turn.

A Special Memory
Kolby Frazier
Blackman Elementary School, Grade 2

One time when my brother was five he stuck his head in a birthday cake! It was his fifth birthday, and his party was at the bowling center. He invited a lot of people. It was packed and lots of people were bowling. It was noisy, too. When we bowled, he won and they drew his name out of a bowl and we all got free pizza! The pizza was delicious but everybody ate all of it up in three straight minutes! My brother ate three pieces of pepperoni pizza, but peeled off the yummy pepperoni. I said, "I will eat them," but he gave them to my older brother. I won an Elmo for him because he likes Elmo. I won it out of the claw machine. He even got to bring home a bowling pin! It was a good birthday party, even if it wasn't mine!

A Special Holiday
Ben Godwin
McFadden School of Excellence, Grade 3

My grandmother has a way with Christmas. She is the oldest of the family. She always decides where our family will celebrate Christmas. It is usually at my cousin's house.

One year, my grandmother was getting tired of having Christmas at my cousin's house. She said she wanted to have it at her house. Her house is fifty years old and tiny. Everyone in the family thought this was a horrible idea. Her living room is the biggest room in her house, but it is loaded with junk. We agreed to the plan though.

On Christmas Eve, my family walked through the door. There were presents of all shapes and sizes in the living room. She had moved her junk to the side (with a lot of help from my Uncle Eric)! It was the best Christmas ever! We were all sorry to doubt her.

The Wedding Day
Dianna Bartilson
Blackman Elementary School, Grade 2

One early fall morning I woke up and I said to myself, "Today is my Aunt Tiffany's wedding day!" I got up and got dressed in a beautiful dress. It had flowers on it, and it was very fluffy. We went to the wedding. I wanted to be the flower girl, but I couldn't. After the wedding, we ate vanilla cake and we drank ice-cold yellow punch. Next, the children played tag and hide and seek. Then we went to our motel and took a nap for a long time. Later, we woke up and went to eat dinner. We ate American food and it was delicious! Then we went to bed for the night. I had a wonderful day.

I Can Still Remember
Allison Keener
Walter Hill Elementary School, Grade 4

I can still remember the days that you lived

The Sundays we spent together, the Saturdays we laughed.

I wish you were still here.

I wish I could see you.

I wish I could hug you.

I can still remember the days I spent with you.

When I Grow Up
Shelby Langford
Blackman Elementary School, Grade 2

When I grow up, I want to be a dancer. I have been dancing for three years and already have my first trophy. This year I am taking a ballet and jazz class. I have also had tap. Dancing makes me proud! I like to be moving instead of sitting around. When I see other people dancing like in theme parks or shows, I want to be dancing too! Maybe one day I will dance in a movie. I love to dance!

My Brother!
Autumn Harris
Roy Waldron School, Grade 5

My most important memory is when I lost my brother at Opry Mills! It wasn't that long ago. In fact, it was just four days ago.

I was spending the day with my stepfather. We went to the ice cream store. While we were waiting in line, I asked my little brother what kind of ice cream he wanted. He didn't answer. That's when I knew something was wrong! I looked back to see what was wrong. He wasn't there!

We looked everywhere. We looked in the shoe store we had stopped in, but he wasn't there. We looked in the magic store. He wasn't there! So I stopped and thought, "What would my brother do?" I told my step dad to keep looking and check out the video game room. I would head back to the ice cream shop. There he was, looking for us! I was so relieved! I NEVER want to lose my brother again!

Belle Aire

Sam Loyd
Blackman Elementary School, Grade 2

My church is a great church. We have a lot of college kids and teachers. The music is so good. On Sunday, we eat donuts at the AO space. That's what they call the college area. The donuts are glazed.

Last Sunday, we ate ice cream and pie. It was so good and cold. Then we slimed Bro Joe. Bro Joe is a preacher at Blastoff Worship. He got slimed because there were 200 kids there. They did it outside on the grass. It was the best Blastoff Worship ever.

Artwork by Autumn Jones, Blackman Elementary School, Grade 2

To Stacey
Jacob S. Van Ekelenburg
Holloway High School, Grade 12

When I gaze into your eyes
I see galaxies reflecting off moonbeams
A swirling mass of complexity
And this to me is what love seems.

When I contemplate your soul
All it does is confuse me
I'll never understand you
So little do you let me see.

When I think of your heart
Though callused, scarred, and beaten
Beating ever so steadily
Never seeming to weaken.

When I face your strength
I know you'll always be there
To hold me up in the light
And show me that you care.

While I write this poem
And try to tell you how I feel
Know that words cannot describe
This friendship filled with zeal.

You are the best friend
I could ever ask for
I just want you to know
And understand for sure.

I hope I can do the same for you
To catch you when you fall
To be the best friend I can be
To keep you standing tall.

My Cat
Caroline Wells
Blackman Elementary School, Grade 2

  I had a cat, but it died. It got hit by a car. I remember the thing he loved the most, our white chair. He always climbed on the back of the chair and made it fall over.
  He always loved to go outside, and when he came in he was usually stinky. He liked to take naps, and when he took a nap he always purred. I remember he loved to play with his cat toys. I remember his claws too! One time my sister was squatting down in front of the hallway. My cat was in the back of the hallway, and ran and jumped on the back of my sister's head. He scratched her.
  My cat's name was Cotton. I got a new cat and named it Mia. I love Mia, but I still love Cotton.

Daddy's Girl
Amy Graham
Siegel High School, Grade 11

I carried the teddy bear you gave me at four,
And cuddled with him while you were out on the road.
I cried when you would leave,
And I smiled when you would come back to me.

From dance lessons to a hunting license,
I have always wanted to be like you.
From orange and camouflage to cowboy boots and wrangler jeans,
Because you wore them, too.

Now it's all pick-up trucks and FFA stuff.
We don't get to hang out much,
Because both our lives have gotten pretty tough.

Even when boyfriends came to call,
You have always been the only man there to help me through it all.
And even when you have to give me away,
I want you to know that I may never be that innocent thing in pigtails anymore,
But I will always be Daddy's little girl!

Christmas
Chad Perkins
Blackman Middle School, Grade 6

One of my most favorite times of year is Christmas. The reason I like it is because of my memories at that time of year. When I was little, I used to live in an apartment with only my mom. We were not very rich. On Christmas, I didn't get much, but one Christmas, I got shaving cream. I loved to play with it!

Soon, it was like a tradition to get shaving cream each year. To this day, I still get shaving cream.

The Beach
Abigail Phonygamy
Walter Hill Elementary School, Grade 2

The beach is really peaceful and quiet. The beautiful seagulls glide in the air. Big waves go back and forth on the sand. The air smells sweet and clean. I rest on the brown sand. It slips through my hands when I pick it up. I go to sleep lying in the sand. It was a good day at the beach.

My Cousin's Baby Brother
Samuel Pitts
Smyrna Primary School, Grade 2

It was Christmas and it took place at my second grandma's house. My cousin's mommy just had a baby. He had a lot of red hair. They named him Tyler. I got to hold him, but only for a few seconds. Then he threw-up on me. It was gross. That was the best and funniest time of my life!

Memories
Autumn Campbell
Lascassas Elementary School, Grade 5

My first loose tooth –
Everyday I tried to pull out my tooth
My friends helped me figure out how to pull it out
Oh, but sooner or later it must come out
When I went to my Aunt Cindy's house
It came out.
Everybody looked at my bloody tooth.
Someday again I'll lose another tooth.

My First Christmas
Rosanny Brito
Smyrna Primary School, Grade 2

My first Christmas was when I was four years old and I ws excited because it was my favorite month and I got what I always wanted. It was a laptop, guitar, and radio. My radio played hip hop, old school, Spanish music. My laptop has fun games on it like math, spelling, and vocabulary games. When I played my guitar, I played it very nicely. It was the best Christmas ever!

The Sound of Laughter
Kaitlin Beck
Oakland High School, Grade 9

    I remember the fall my family and I moved into our first home, which smelled of just-dry plaster and too new carpet. The sacred threshold was an all but inviting atmosphere to a third-grader, being protected tooth and nail with food, footwear, and all things childish. After the first week, our sanctuary had become a plague; my mother first coaxed, then commanded me to play outdoors where I would not be such a nuisance.

    I had not looked favorably upon my surroundings thus far but ushered outside in wool and mittens. I began to view my new outdoors favorably. I remember the way the chill fall winds had an "Autumn in Vermont" way of whisking the leaves around, which charmed me. Busying myself by tossing armfuls of leaves over my head, I can remember being interrupted by her laughter. Surprised into rest, and listening intently, I was drawn to her. I followed the sound of her voice, half-mesmerized. It was a sweet, thick trail of music; the sagging, overgrown barbed wire I passed was not dangerous or foreboding, but exciting and tantalizing. I crossed through the dense thicket of chest-high grasses, and it seemed as if the sound of her happiness made a path of entrancing melody for me to follow. The crisp, biting air brought a blush to my nose and cheeks and tousled my hair, but that was the way she first saw me. I remember first seeing her. The water pushed over her soft warm banks in an untamed modesty, and the delightful gurgle it produced was still sweeter to me than on the trail. Gray, skeletal trees lined her banks and made her even more majestic; a queen of her court. I spent the rest of the afternoon far into dusk, wondering at her unabashed beauty.

    I can't remember the second in time, exactly, but through the hours I sat on her banks, I do remember feeling her wrap her arms around me, enveloping me. As we made delicate yet powerful connections, almost like silvery, spider-silk, I was unable to leave entirely. A large part of my heart I gave to her, and I am sure it can be found still, floating in that river.

Reflections
Jonathan Mullins
Smyrna High School, Grade 12

Looking back on times we had,
Through the good and the bad.
To all the thoughts that made you mad.
These are my reflections.

The memories we shared together,
Through the veils and stormy weather.
Also in times we enjoyed each other.
These are my reflections.

The way you looked into my eyes,
Through all your toils and your sighs.
I always remained near your side.
These are my reflections.

The way you never seemed to care,
The way I sat with empty chair.
You never seemed to be right there.
These are my reflections.

Now its over, now it's through,
Because of the many things you choose.
Our time together was for us to lose.
These are my reflections.

Looking back it all seems clear,
I'll hold these emotions very dear.
However, it seems the time is near.
To close all my reflections.

About My Seventh Birthday
Alexandra Cunfidd
Smyrna Primary School, Grade 2

My favorite memory was my seventh birthday party at Chucky Cheese. My aunt got me a guitar. It was so cool. When I opened it, I played it right away. Everybody liked the song I played. It was the best moment of my life! Also, the cake and ice cream were delicious. After the party, we went home and had another party.

The Best Ball Game
Tyler Beck
Roy Waldron School, Grade 3

I went to Cookeville and went to our hotel. I had to get ready for my baseball game. It was the state tournament, and I was excited. To pass the time away we went swimming. Next we rode my friend's new bike, then we ate pizza and we went to bed. The next morning we got up and got dressed. Then we drove to the ball field a mile away. We went on the field and the umpire said, "Play ball." Then they popped it up to Mario at catcher. He caught it. It was one out. The next batter hit it to me. I touched the bag, and I threw it to second base, and I got us three outs. It was our turn to bat and next *MARIO* was up to bat. He got a double. It was my turn to bat. Then I got a double which made Mario go to home plate. Then that made us **win** the game.

My First Christmas
Lexus Saunders
Smyrna Primary School, Grade 2

My favorite memory was Christmas when I was five years old. I got a Britney Spears CD. Also, I got a bicycle and a doll house. After that I gave my mom and my dad a hug. I was so happy that I ran around the house That was the best Christmas ever!

Baseball
Kinley Seaborn
Blackman Elementary School, Grade 5

The first touch of homeplate against my cleat felt great.
Looking at the diamond-shaped field was like looking at gold.
When I run around the bases it clears my mind.
Every bad thought goes away.

My Favorite Memory
Crawford Swafford
Smyrna Primary School, Grade 2

My favorite memory was when my sister and I went to the park. My sister taught me to ride a bike. I was going so fast I wanted to race her. Then I crashed into a tree. Last, I fell off and started to cry. She picked me and the bike up. My sister said, "Are you all right?" I said, "Yes." I will never forget my sister helping me ride a bike.

A Wonderful Place
Emily Sumners
Thurman Francis Arts Academy, Grade 8

Down a curvy, rocky road,
There is a place I'm blessed to know.
Where time stops in its tracks;
I promise you there is nothing it lacks.
The smell of country fills the air.
That place is just short of heaven, I swear.
With the clear blue sky and the sun shining down,
And stubby green grass covering the ground,
We walk to the church in afternoon hours;
On the way picking Nana some wild flowers.
My grandpa is sitting outside with his dog.
My cousins and I are singing a song.
Although we sing so very off key,
I'm with my family and that makes me happy.
As we sit at the table to pray,
I think to myself, "What a wonderful day!"
I wish it could stay this way,
For things to be this wonderful everyday.
But soon I will go back home,
And I will look forward to the next time I come.
I hate to say good-bye to this wonderful place.
Who knew something could be so beautiful in an empty space?

Chapter Four

Connecting through Family Memories

My Special Family
Brock Baker
McFadden School of Excellence, Grade 4

My family is very, very special
Wonderful and proud
My family is so big
And we speak it aloud.

If my family were not here
I don't know what I would do
Sitting around lonely
Really sad and blue.

My family is always there for me
When I need them the most
Like when I'm hungry
And I need some hot breakfast toast.

When I'm at my sporting events
They are cheering for me
Run, run is what they say
Then they cheer "Hooray, hooray!"

Now that I am ten
Growing so, so fast
They want to put a brick on me
So that I will last.

When I go to college
When I go away
They will ask me
Will you please stay?

I will have children of my own
So young and new
But I will always remember
My family, I love you.

Connection Flag
Logan Coffey
Wilson Elementary School, Grade 5

My connection of the heart
Is the flag I got
When my Papa passed away.
And I keep that flag in my room,
And every time I walk in my room
I look at it and think of him.

Daddy
Mary Katherine Bogle
Blackman Middle School, Grade 8

Daddy. The world reminds people of many special memories. The world means everything to me. Daddies can always fix and build anything. Whenever I look at my dad, I see a man who can do anything. The grease under his fingernails from working on airplanes and drag cars. His eyes always with the look of love and carefulness in them. His mind, always pondering on the thought of new inventions. His hands with the roughness touch, but when you touch them, you get a feeling that he would never hurt you. Daddy cares for everything and everyone. I know that when I look at him, I have the best Daddy of all.
Thank you Mom and Dad for everything you've blessed me with!

Holiday Cheer
Kayleigh Barnes
Wilson Elementary School, Grade 1

Holidays are special to me because of my family. It makes me feel safe, happy, and loved when I am with my family. My favorite thing to do with them is eat! There is always somebody giggling and laughing while playing games. I am thankful for my family. I know in my heart my family will always love me.

Family
Harris Smith
Thurman Francis Arts Academy, Grade 4

Family, family, you are not bad.

Without you I'd be so very sad.

Sometimes I make you very mad,

But when I am with you, I'm very glad.

I Love My Uncle
Kyle Herndon
Blackman Elementary School, Grade 3

I have an uncle, his name is Tim.
He is really nice and I love him.

The war in Iraq is taking him away.
He is leaving soon to fight for the U.S.A.
To keep us safe and our country free,
He will fight to protect you and me.
Uncle Tim will do whatever he can.
He is a strong and proud man.

He likes to play and run with us.
He even loves us when we fuss.
Uncle Tim has a wife and two sons.
It is Aunt Crissy, Taylor, and Mason.

When he comes home, we will be glad.
Then Crissy, Taylor, and Mason won't be sad.
I can't wait to play with him,
For he is special…my Uncle Tim.

Family
Ashley Stanton
Thurman Francis Arts Academy, Grade 6

A family connects one person to another,
Like from your mom to your brother,
A family is made of people that you love and care for,
For your family there will always be an open door,
A family connects a cousin to an aunt,
Or a father to his daughter,
My family is made of the people I love and always will,
I know they'll watch over me if I become ill,
You should always let your family know,
That you love them so,
Because you might not have another day to do this,
So give them a kiss,
And wish a sweet wish,
Remember a friend is a friend,
They come and they go,
But a family will be there high and low.

The Best Mommy
Victoria Alexander
Wilson Elementary School, Grade 1

She is the best mommy in the world because she is kind. She keeps me safe when I am scared. My mommy has the best smile and my mommy has special kisses that heal my boo-boos. She is also my best friend and I love her very much.

Wrapped in Your Arms
Ukyeye Wilt
McFadden School of Excellence, Grade 8

As I entered the world, people standing around me,
You held me close and I felt safe.

Of course, we've had some disagreements,
But every night when I'm about to go to bed,
You hold me close and I feel safe.

When I walk down the aisle and make such a big step in my life,
I know that you will be there
To hold me and make me feel safe.

You have always loved me and always will,
And when the time comes to help you,
I will hold you and make you feel safe.

My New Baby Sister
Christopher Patton
Blackman Elementary School, Grade 3

When I heard we were getting a baby
I thought I'd like her maybe.
Would she be big and bald?
By what name would she be called?
Would she be black or white?
Will she be a fright and bite?

I remember the day we brought her home
Because I jumped right on the phone
As she rocked and rocked in her crib,
Then she burped in her bib.
After she goes to sleep,
She snores and kicks her feet.

Impact
Lisa Calabrese
Siegel High School, Grade 10

I think about your smile, then I imagine your grimace of agony
I think about your generosity, then I remember how your life was taken away
I think about your laugh, then I try to block out the cries of your last hour
But then I think about your courage, and I remember the people you faced and the cause
      you stood for
I think about your joy, and I know you're waiting for me in Heaven
I think about your teachings on life, then I realize the greatest example you showed me:
You lost your life trying to help others gain theirs.

My Hero, My Grandfather
William Gaines
Blackman Elementary School, Grade 3

    I was one year old when I met my grandfather. He stood very tall. My grandfather was a very strong man who was always to the point. My grandfather was my hero above any other. My grandfather became sick when I was three. During that time he lost one leg. That was the thing about my grandfather—he never gave up. He stayed by himself. He cooked his own food, and for us also. My grandfather was a very remarkable man.
    On June 20, 2003, I lost my hero. That was the biggest change of my life, to be eight years old, and have to say goodbye to one of the strongest people that I have ever met. One thing my grandfather left me was to always believe, trust, treat others the way you wish to be treated, and never give up.
    That was my hero, my grandfather, George Wade.

My Sister Maddy
Chelsea Williams
Rockvale Elementary School, Grade 5

My name is Chelsea Dawn Williams, and I have a two-year-old sister named Madelyn Grace Williams. Before my sister Maddy was born, she had many problems. In this story, I am going to tell you about Maddy's problems and the miracle she came to be. I will also tell you how Maddy's birth changed me and how thankful I am my sister lived. She is very special to me. I hope you enjoy the story of my sister, how she was near death and what she does now.

Maddy had many problems before birth. First, when my mom went to the doctor, we found out Maddy had seven cists in her brain. Cists are like little knots. Maddy had seven! Then, when we returned to the doctor again, the seven cists (knots) were gone! We were very excited! The bad thing was, we found out Maddy could be a waterhead! Which means, she had a lot of fluid (water and yucky stuff) built up in her brain. I was so upset! After that, she was clear of being a waterhead, but now she might have Edward Syndrome! That was the worst! My mom burst into tears! Later, I found out Edward Syndrome meant she would die before she was born or two weeks after she was born! I was terribly overcome! I cried for hours. A few weeks later, we went back to the doctor, she was clear of Edward Syndrome! I was happier than ever! The only thing we didn't know was if she would be born with Down Syndrome. That means she would be a little slower at learning than others.

My family and I were told cute little Maddy would be born January 5, 2003. We had about two months left before she was born. We could hardly bear it!

Finally, it was delivery day! I felt big! I was finally going to be a big sister! As I sat in the boring, quiet waiting room with Gran and Granddaddy, I suddenly saw nurses and the doctor rush into the room where my mom was! Then we heard a little cry. It was Maddy! When I saw her she took my breath. She looked perfect! Every baby gets a score from 1-10, to see if they are healthy; my sister got a 9.9. She was perfect! She had big rosy cheeks, a tiny button nose, itty bitty, sour, puckering lips, and brown hair, with a cowlick in the front.

Maddy is two years old now. She has blonde hair, hazel eyes, big cheeks, and a cowlick up front. Maddy's favorite toy is a bear. Our aunt and uncle made him for her at the Build A Bear Factory when she was a newborn. His name is really silly. It's Boo Bear. Maddy talks a lot, but she's a girl! I tried to keep up with all the words she said when she was only one! Maddy says words like bubble, Mamma, Daddy, sissy, or sometimes Chessy, which means Chelsea. Her reactions with the family are pretty good. Her reactions with me aren't always so good, but I'm not always so good to her either. Yet, you gotta love her.

My sister has helped me be thankful for what I have. Before, I used to dwell about what I didn't have. Today when I start to worry, I think of Maddy, my miracle baby. People say I am Maddy's hero because I'm bigger, but she's really my hero. Nobody will ever know how truly blessed I am.

Connections
Shawn Cannon
Blackman Elementary School, Grade 3

      I went to my uncle's house; he lives in North Carolina. I saw my family at my uncle's house. My family and I went to dinner. I saw half of my family there. I played video games then I ate dinner with my family. After dinner we went back to my uncle's house and I went to bed. In the morning, I got up and put my clothes on and my family and I went to the beach. I played with my uncle and my brother. I went surfing and fell a lot. I went snorkeling and it was really fun. I saw lots of fish and no sharks. I got in the car and went back home. My brother cried too hard, and he got a headache. When we got home, I took a nap. I was worn out.

Why!
Zach Ritter
Roy Waldron School, Grade 4

Well, it all started back when I was three. My parents always argued. When I was four, it happened. They split up! So my mom got me and my brother and two sisters. My dad got an apartment. So I got to see my dad on weekends. When I was five, I started school. My dad got a girlfriend. Next she was his fiancée. But she was bad and they broke up. When I was six, I had no idea I would only have a few more months with my mom and brother. I was still six and the funeral came. At least the last word I ever said to them was "Bye" because they were going somewhere. Then a mobile home crashed into them. About two weeks later was the funeral. When I was eight, my uncle died. At least the last word I got to say to him was "Bye."

My Brother and Me
Kacee Pieratt
Blackman Elementary School, Grade 5

My brother is a special part of my life.
He is really, really nice.
We don't always fight,
But sometimes we might.
I love him and he loves me.
That's the way it's always gonna be!

In Loving Memory of Daddy
Mandy Reeves
Eagleville High School, Grade 9

Daddy,

God looked around His garden and found an empty place.
He then looked down upon the earth and saw your tired face.
He put his arms around you and lifted you to rest
God's garden must be beautiful, He only takes the best.
It broke my heart to lose you, but you did not go
For part of me went with you the day God called you home.

My Little Brother
Tyler Bouttavong
Blackman Elementary School, Grade 3

I have a little brother
His name is Hunter
He screams like a hyena
He chirps like a bird.
He likes to run around
and follows me like a crazy clown.
But I still love him.

And I Remember
Jessica Shelkey
Eagleville High School, Grade 9

Sitting on the back porch
A hummingbird flies by
And I remember.
Light pours through the door
And you, Grandpa, take your last breath
The door slams shut
And all standing around
Look to the door
Where a single bird hovers
One small, lone hummingbird
Small, yes, but full of meaning
It hovers back and forth
Between the two panes of glass
As if saying
"Don't cry for me, I'm all right."
And I remember.
The beating of wings when the bird flies by
"He's sending us a sign,"
My Grandmother cries.
And I do believe
That the bird was a sign from above
Not a single one, all year
My grandmother's favorite bird
He sent it
And, I remember.

Connection to My Grandpa
Cass Jones
Smyrna Elementary School, Grade 2

Dear Grandpa Ray,

I know I never knew you, however Christian has told me all about you. He says that the blue bear in Grandma's room is made of your shirt. Grandpa, they tell me you died when you got so sick. I feel very sad, because I've heard about how nice you were, but I never met you. I have been told that you were the nicest man in our family. I believe this is a true statement. Your pictures show a kind and smiling face.

Love,
Cass

God Just Couldn't Resist Her
Amy Cochran
Eagleville High School, Grade 9

Thirteen years have gone by since you haven't been by my side.
What's funny is even though you're gone, a piece of you still lives on.
Sometimes I'll look up at the stars and wonder where in heaven exactly you are.
I'd reach as far as the moon is hung, and scream 'till there is no more air left
        in my lungs.
Just to have you one more day, just to have one more chance to play.
People say you don't know what love is when you're young, but I think they're wrong.
How can they say that when we had a friendship so strong?
When we were little we were inseparable.
Yes, we would fight, but you have to admit that's life.
I'm sad that you had to go, but I'm glad that my love for you still glows.
It's hard to think that I lost a sister, but I know that God just couldn't resist her!

My Grandpa and I
Roxanna Bustillo
Smyrna Elementary School, Grade 2

My grandpa is my best friend. He is thirty-eight and I love him. At night before dinner, Grandpa and I sit on the couch and he reads me books like Arthur. Once Grandpa took me to the fair. He won me a little Pooh bear. We had popcorn and coke. He rode the fireball with me. We spun around really fast! We were dizzy! Grandpa also takes me to the park. We play tag but he doesn't catch me. He pushes me up to the sky on the swings! My grandpa is in my heart forever.

My Mama
Isaac Haley
Eagleville School, Grade 3

    My mama is so special. She cares for me always, especially when I am sick. She cooks for me. She buys the best clothes for me. She talks to me when I am down. Best of all, she prays for me and kisses me everyday. She loves me. "I love my mama!"

My Dad
Rodney Schade
Smyrna Elementary School, Grade 2

    My dad is my best friend. He lets me play outside after I do my chores. Dad takes me to K-Mart to buy school clothes. We play Monopoly together. He usually wins. We also play Go Fish. Dad and I like to watch the Titans play on TV. He brings me to school everyday. I do what he says. When I'm with Daddy, I feel safe.

Dad
Adrianna Moss
Smyrna Primary School, Grade 4

Loveable
Huggable
Silly
Sings
Plays guitar
Good cook
Good parent
Picks on me
Loves me
Will be with me always
My dad.

How I Became a Chef
Billie Danielle Walden
Smyrna Elementary School, Grade 5

One sunny morning as I was getting up for breakfast, the smell of crisp bacon led me to the kitchen. Mama was making her delicious, homemade, blueberry pancakes. Mama knows how to cook anything you could think of, and that's how I learned to cook. She has taught me how to cook everything. Every morning and every night, we have cooked together from pancakes in the morning to casseroles at night. I admire her a whole lot. She encourages me to do anything I want, and that's how I became a chef.

David, My Brother, My Hero
Zachary Green
Smyrna Primary School, Grade 4

My brother is in the Army, and he is my hero. I will always look up to him because he went to Iraq to help other people be free. Even though he is back at Fort Campbell now, he has to stay ready for battle. He is training to go back to Iraq. I pray that maybe someday, everything that David and all the other soldiers are fighting for (freedom, peace, and happiness) will come true. I believe all soldiers are heroes, but David is my number one hero. I'm very proud of my brother, my hero.

My Childhood
Mallory Pawlik
Blackman Elementary School, Grade 4

When I was little, my life was hard. My parents split apart. I still remember the day my dad left. I was lying in bed and I heard my mom and dad fighting. I started to cry. I ran into their room and my dad was gone. My mom picked me up and said, "I love you."

I ran to the door and looked out the window. I saw my dad's van at the stop sign and then he took off.

Now I am older and I have both a new step-mom and a step-dad. It is a little hard because my dad lives in Texas, and I live with my mom in Tennessee. My mom works for Continental Airlines, so I fly to Texas every other weekend to see my dad.

I love both my parents so much and I wish they were still together. But life is how it has to be, and it is the way it is. That's how life works sometimes. I am happy now.

Thank You
Chelsa Read
Thurman Francis Arts Academy, Grade 6

No one knows how much they do,
It's way too much to handle for two.

They praise you when you've acted good,
And punish when they think they should.

Mom cleans your clothes and cooks your food,
And puts up with you when you're in a bad mood.

Dad does his best and mostly succeeds,
He encourages you to write and to read.

They make you feel special in every situation,
They talk to you, quite honest communication.

They want you to try your best in everything you do,
They always help you out, and together you pull through.

They love you always with all their heart,
And they tell everyone that you're so smart.

They listen to you when you are happy and sad,
So take the time to say, "Thanks, Mom and Dad!"

Appreciation
Angela Leyhew
Oakland High School, Grade 10

Thanks for giving me life and paving my road into the future.
Thanks for changing my diapers and wiping my runny nose.
Thanks for reading me stories and helping put those puzzles together.
Thanks for giving me everything I've wanted and grounding me whenever I back-talked.
Thanks for still loving me even after you spanked me.
Thanks for being my friends and not only my parents.
Thanks for standing by me through everything and giving me all the love in the world.
Thanks for the sacrifices you've given just so I could do what I wanted.
Most of all thank you for being there and being the best parents I could ever dream of.
If it weren't for you two, I wouldn't have the chances and opportunities that you may not have had.
Thank you! I love you more than anything and with all my heart.

Dear Brother
Leanna McClintock
Lascassas Elementary School, Grade 4

Dear Brother,

I know that you are going away to college soon, and I think that everyone in the family is sad about it. I hope that you will come and visit us when you can. I also hope that you like college, and even though you can't wait to go, I will really miss you.

Good luck!

Love,
Leanna

My Dad Is Special
Jaylee Oliver
McFadden School of Excellence, Grade 1

My dad is special because he plays with me. He is special because he loves me!
When I am hurt, my dad helps me. He plays soccer with me.
My dad will always be there when I need him!

My Grandma
Cody West
Lascassas Elementary School, Grade 4

My Grandma is very special because…

She is as playful as a puppy,
As nice as a new corvette,
As cool as the winter snow, and
As special as a Lamborghini!

That is why I love my grandma!

Dedicated to my grandmother, Christin West
With love from Cody West

A Special Time
Kirstin Taylor
McFadden School of Excellence, Grade 1

A special time in my life is when my baby sister was born. Her eyes were very squinty and she screamed her head off. It was still fun because I got to go to a friend's house.

My Brother Grayson
Taylor Rigsby
Lascassas Elementary School, Grade 4

I remember the day that my brother Grayson was born. He was born on June 19, 2002, at 4:21 P.M. The only thing I kept saying was, I didn't think he'd look like that." He was cute and he still is cute. Grayson looks just like my daddy. He has light blond hair. He has blue eyes. He's about three feet tall. He is now two years old and loves the Wiggles. He's talking a lot and putting words in sentences.

I love my brother. He bothers me sometimes and hurts me sometimes, but I forgive him. He goes to pre-school two days a week and loves it. He loves to sing and dance and play his guitar. He also loves Sesame Street. He has a lot of their characters. He loves to eat chicken nuggets, mashed potatoes, corn, peas, pears, and candy. He loves tractors. He likes lawnmowers, too. Now you know about my brother. He's the best little brother in the world.

My Special Person
Trey McAdams
McFadden School of Excellence, Grade 1

My special person is my brother. I chose him because he loves me. He plays with me. He chases me. He jumps on me. He eats with me. He is my buddy. He is the best person! I like him, too. He is fun.

Thank You, Jim
Dustin Mears
Lascassas Elementary School, Grade 4

November 16, 2004

Dear Jim,
      Thank you for all that you taught me, like riding a bike and writing cursive. You are the coolest brother that I have ever had, Jim. I love you in a brother way.

From your brother,
Dash or Dustin

The Mother's Day Plate
MaryGrace Bouldin
Homer Pittard Campus School, Kindergarten

I was only three years old when I made my mommy a Mother's Day plate. I put my handprint on a plate and put a dot in the middle. I went there with my pre-school class. I did it at The Artistic Cafe. I made it because it was close to Mother's Day. I put two big dots on the side of the plate. It was a glass plate so if you had it, you would have to be very careful so it does not break. I made this plate because I love my Mommy because she tucks me in the bed and reads me a story every night and she gives me carrots every day.
The End.

Mother Deary
Nicky Balduf
Siegel High School, Grade 10

I'm sorry mother deary!
For breaking curfew the other night
And slipping that bite or five of casserole to the dog
I'm afraid I forgot to mention my report card…
Oh, and you know your favorite vase?
It just so happens I misplaced my cell phone
I mean, uh, it was stolen yesterday
Oops, Aunt Nancy called for you
She said it was important!
I may not have fed the cat this morning
And well, could you pick me up at five?
I love you mother deary!

My Baby Sister
Kristen Barnes
Wilson Elementary School, Grade 2

When my baby sister was born I was so excited! I had to stay at my grandparent's house for two days. When we got to the hospital we had to stand outside the door. Finally, we heard crying. I was the first to get to see her. She was so cute. We named her Courtney. When we got home I got to feed her a bottle. I am happy I have a baby sister.

My Family
Julia Durant
LaVergne Primary School, Grade 2

My family is special to me. I love them. They keep me safe. They play with me. I help my Mom with my baby brother. I love my family.

My Twin Brothers
Zachary Fussell
Wilson Elementary School, Grade 4

Twins
Sweet, cute
Crying, talking, smiling
Bottles, blankets, boys, babies
Crawling, laughing, sleeping
Funny, loveable
Twins

My Grandpa
Patrick Stanford
Wilson Elementary School, Grade 4

Goes to do what has to be done
Respects other people
Always goes wherever we go
Nicer than anybody else in my family
Does whatever he has to do
People in my family love him a lot
All of us in my family respect him for what he does for us.

I Am

Ashley Thompson
LaVergne Middle School, Grade 7

I am a fun and loveable daughter
I wonder what my dad is doing in war
I hear my dad say he loves me
I see my dad coming home soon
I want my dad to be safe
I am a fun and loveable daughter.

I pretend that my dad is home
I feel my dad's love
I touch the letters that my dad writes to me
I worry that my dad is in danger
I cry when my dad leaves for war
I am a fun and loveable daughter.

I understand that my dad has to go to war when he is told to
I say that my dad is the bravest dad ever
I dream about my dad in war
I try to be the bravest to see my dad go
I hope my dad is all right
I am a fun and loveable daughter.

Grandmother

Mayra Campusano
Wilson Elementary School, Grade 4

Gentle as a rose
Respectful
Always so kind
Nice as a butterfly
Dancing in the sunlight
Memories are warm
Over in heaven
Tenderly we cry
Hours of good times
Enjoyed her laughter
Remembering her.

My Family
Brendan Willis
LaVergne Primary School, Grade 2

My family loves me. My family gets me food. My family tucks me in. My family takes care of me. They give us medicine when we need it.

My Mom
Eli Clutter
McFadden School of Excellence, Grade 3

My mom is very special to me. She was the best and I loved her a lot. She taught pre-school. My mom and I loved to plant flowers. We did it every day. My sister and I would put lotion on her back and then draw something in the lotion. Mom would have to guess what it was.

Then on June 17, 2001, she died of a blood clot that hit her brain. I was only five and she died. She died on Father's Day. I'll always miss her. I'll always have a place in my heart for her. I'll never forget her. I love you, Mom.

Uncle
Caroline Love
Walter Hill Elementary School, Grade 3

Uncle
Energetic, clever
Playing, laughing, farming
What a great life!
Working camping, watching
Generous, respectful
Jeffery Love.

Grammy and Grampa
Caitlin Meier
McFadden School of Excellence, Grade 3

My grammy and grampa were so nice. I am thankful for them. They always would hug and kiss me. I love them a lot.

My grampa died two years ago. I really miss him. He always took me on a walk. He told me that if something tried to hurt me, he would hit it with his walking stick. I love him.

My grammy died in May 2004. I miss her a lot! She always took me shopping. I love her. She always got me pretty stuff.

These next holidays will be hard without Grammy and Grampa. But, I know they love us a lot! We love them too.

Mother
Austin Roden
Walter Hill Elementary School, Grade 3

Mother
Beautiful, respectful
Cooking, cleaning, playing
She's a good mother!
Planting, working, teaching
Cool, trustworthy
Tonya

When I Go with Papa
Allie Nadeau
McFadden School of Excellence, Grade 2

When I go with Papa, we go to the farm. When we get there, we mow the grass. Then we feed the turkeys. Papa gave two turkeys to me for my birthday. I will never eat them. Next we feed the cows. Sometimes we jump on hay bales. When the day is over, I am tired but I am happy.

Aubrey's Family
Aubrey Kenney
Walter Hill Elementary School, Grade 1

I love my family so much.

My family is so much fun

and my family loves me, too.

We are a great family.

What a great family we are.

My Family
Kaitlyn Palmer
Lascassas Elementary School, Grade 3

> My family I love,
> They always give me hugs.
> My mom, my sis, my dad, my cats,
> They all love me just like that!
> We do everything together,
> No matter what the weather!
> My family I love.

A Special Person
Amanda Pratt
Blackman Elementary School, Grade 2

    I love to go to my grandma's house. I always see her cooking potatoes. I can almost taste the gravy. I love her gravy!
    I love to sew with Grandma. We sew all kinds of stuff, like quilts. We also play tea party or restaurant. I am a waiter. She is a customer. My grandma pretends her dog is crying when he barks, like he is a baby.
    I say, "Aw, man," when it is time to go. Then we say our good-byes. Before we leave, I say, "I love you, and I will love you forever."

My Last Family Christmas Memory

Misty Davenport
Eagleville High School, Grade 9

Do you have a memory that just sticks in your head like no other? Well I do. Mine is the Christmas of 2002. What made it so special? This was the last Christmas my family was together. I know that sounds a little silly, but to me it is very special.

My sister, Alicia, and I woke up around seven in the morning. We ran into our mom and dad's room. Of course they were already up; they always were up first. I think sometimes they were more excited than we were.

We all went into the living room. They always made us wait a little while. Daddy made a fire and Mama put in the Elvis Christmas CD. We all sat down, and one by one Mama would hand Alicia and me presents. Even if we did not like them much we would act like we did anyway. Mama and Daddy always did try so very hard to give us all they could. Even if they did not get anything they always got us something.

Afterwards, we would sit there and laugh, tell jokes, and just enjoy being a family. I miss those talks so very much. Then we would try on everything and clean up the mess. Mama would cook breakfast and Daddy would sit there and sing Elvis songs. We sat down, said grace, and had our last Christmas breakfast together. That night we said our goodnights and went to bed. I never would have guessed that that would have been our last Christmas or I would have made it better than it already was.

From that day, we spent about three months together as a family. Then my parents got a divorce. That truly ripped my thirteen-year-old heart to pieces. It was not that bad until they brought new people into our lives. I was not used to other people kissing my mama and daddy.

I had to get used to it. There was nothing I could do to change their minds now. So Alicia and I spent Christmas of 2003 with different people. That morning I dreaded getting up. I felt like crying with every rip I took of the wrapping paper. Nothing was the same. No more of Daddy sitting there holding Mama singing, "Here comes Santa Claus." No more of Mama standing by the stove laughing at him. Just everything was wrong. I felt like I was in a different world.

I guess this is how it is going to be. I miss it just being us four, though. My Christmas will never be the same. I will never forget that wonderful Christmas memory of 2002.

All About Mom
Ethan Young
Blackman Elementary School, Grade 2

My mom is thin. She looks pretty. She has smooth skin. She has brown eyes. She feels soft, too.

Mom feeds us. She gets ice cream. She orders pizza. She cooks spaghetti. It feels squishy.

My mom makes us laugh when she tickles me. She tells us good stories about God. She teaches a lot. We learn a lot. Mom helps with homework.

Mom is good to me. She is kind to us. She helps me do all kinds of things. She is my mom forever, and I will love her forever.

I Remember Grandpa
Ashley Wise
Rock Springs Middle School, Grade 7

I remember the smell of cinnamon and spice when Grandpa moved in.
And the way he always complained, "Why won't you take me home?"
I remember the day Grandpa held my baby brother for the first time.
And the way he always sat in his rocking chair and looked at the picture of old Grams.
I remember that day in kindergarten when I came home and Grandpa wasn't there.
And the way I ran through the house screaming, "Where is he? He can't be gone!"
I remember the dark clouds on the day that my mom told me I couldn't go to the
    funeral.
And how the smell of cinnamon slowly dissolved away.
And I remember how Grandpa was gone on that rainy day.

Remember When

Tangelia Cannon
Smyrna High School, Grade 11

Woke up this morning,
Thought about you.
Looked at a picture,
Started to cry.
Memories of laughter,
Tears and happy times,
Rolled through my head.

You are my dad.
The best man in the world.
You loved me,
Held my hand.
Hugged me,
Wiped my tears.
Every day, every night.
Whenever I needed you.
I called your name.
You were there for me.
With a word of wisdom,
Or an arm full of love.

When I was born,
You wrote me a song.
"Born on a Sunday in TN...
My little girl named Tangelia Marie."
You taught me how to ride my first bike.
And when I fell,
You picked me up and gave me a hug.
You made me feel safe,
During the storm.
And before I ran away,
You shut the door.

You are my dad,
The best man in the world.
You loved me,
Held my hand.
Hugged me,
Wiped my tears.
Every day, every night.
Whenever I needed you.
I called your name.
You were there for me.

With a word of wisdom,
Or an arm full of love.

My first year of school,
You came to everything.
When I was the elephant,
You cheered my name.
Then in third grade..
Math happened.
Long division and multiplication.
I didn't understand,
But you were patient.
And during middle high,
When I got sick,
You got off from work,
And took care of me.

You are my dad,
The best man in the world.
You loved me,
Held my hand.
Hugged me,
Wiped my tears.
Every day, every night.
Whenever I needed you.
I called your name.
You were there for me.
With a word of wisdom,
Or an arm full of love.

The sands of time,
Are picking up.
I'm getting older,
And these days are going faster.
The time we spend together,
Grows shorter by the hour.
But the memories,
You've created,
Will stay forever in my heart.
You are my daddy.
And I really love ya.

You are my dad,
The best man in the world.
You loved me,
Held my hand.
Hugged me,
Wiped my tears.

Every day, every night.
Whenever I needed you.
I called your name.
You were there for me.
With a word of wisdom,
Or an arm full of love.

I love you, Daddy.

Sister Poem
Levi Morales
Smyrna Primary School, Grade 2

>   Sister
>   nice, pretty,
>   playing, loving, caring.
>   She makes me happy.
>   Friend

Connections like a Magnet
Logan Caffrey
Roy Waldron School, Grade 4

      The connections of my family are special because they love me and take care of me. I love them because they love me. If I could pick any family in the world I would pick ours because they do so much for me. My sister can be mean at first but once you get to know her you start to have a friend connection with her. She and I have a good sister connection. My family is like a magnet that sticks to a refrigerator. My momma, my daddy, and I have good connections like they tell me to do something and I already know what they are going to say before they even get it out. When they hug me it's like a magnet connecting together. Then here comes my brothers; our connections are playing outside and being nice to each other. But the most important thing to us is connecting!

Special One
Kate Walrath
Siegel Middle School, Grade 8

All I wanted was you.
I didn't expect this.
You knew how to treat me. You would even say to me
"Baby, you mean the world to me."
 Don't you know I miss you? Why did you go so fast?
I can't believe you are in my past.
You had to go on the night that we would share that one special kiss.
A kiss, that I would always miss.

Dedicated to My Grandfather,
David Bernard Walrath, II

My Great-grandma
Cole Woodward
Christiana Middle School, Grade 8

Just one more hug
From that great-grandma of mine,
I promise that I won't
Moan, groan, or at the least even whine.

Yes, that's what I need
I need her here with me,
I want there once
Again to be a "we."

I wish she were here
To be a guide,
She could help me with any feat
No matter how far or wide.

That's all I need
To be fine,
Just one more hug from
That great-grandma of mine.

The Girl Next Door
Katie Shacklett
Siegel High School, Grade 9

The girl next door lived right in my house.
We talked, we joked, we got mad, and we got sad,
She was older, I was bolder.
Life was great with the girl next door.
She grew older, she grew wiser.
We lost touch; we didn't care too much,
Then we remembered all those times,
And all the binds, we cried and,
Then she moved, the girl next door.
The girl was my sister.

Family and Friends
Keira Biggs
Thurman Francis Arts Academy, Grade 8

Family who love you
Are always there.
Moms and dads that care for you,
In happiness or in despair.
Loved ones looking out for you,
You know they're always there.

And even when it seems like
No one really cares
Don't ever give up on them, even if it seems fair.

Forever they will love you,
Remember that their love,
It never really
Ends,
Never regret what you have,
Don't forget what you have,
Savor forever the gift that you have;
      Family and Friends.

My Brother
Morgan Taylor
Siegel High School, Grade 9

I look up to you with admiring eyes,
But you're afraid to meet my stare.
Then you know what you'd have to do,
Admit the feelings are there.
You're scared you will let me down,
And for that you'll never know,
Just how much you influence me,
And the way my life will go.
You're only half a part of me,
But to my heart it is a whole.
You're my brother, my friend, my protector,
And always a small piece of my soul.

She's Here
Kaitlin Hurt
David Youree Elementary School, Grade 5

She's here. She's here.

My sister is here!

The day has come

Her life has begun

Until her days are done.

She's here. She's here.

My sister is here!

Daddy
Chase McBryar
Thurman Francis Arts Academy, Grade 6

When I was a little baby,
My father died.
And I thought "Why?"
I was mad at God for a while
And all my tears were in a pile,
So to this day I don't know why,
Why God picked me to have to cry.

Twins

Chad Russell and Chris Russell
Blackman Middle School, Grade 6

Chad:

My twin and I are best friends. We have been in every class since first grade. His name is Chris.

About a month ago, he moved downstairs. It is great having a room by myself. Sometimes he comes upstairs to watch TV. I guess that is cool.

Sometimes, Chris and I can finish each other's sentences. That is weird. My brother will always be my friend.

Chris:

I have a connection with my brother. He has always been there for me. I don't know what I would do without him. He is my twin. We have done everything together. We get angry at each other every now and then. It's OK. Brothers do that. For eleven years, we have been through thick and thin. He will always be my brother.

Artwork by Kelsey Dearmon, Thurman Francis Arts Academy, Grade 6

My Mom
Erin Paul
Thurman Francis Arts Academy, Grade 5

She is . . .
A lady who became a friend
A great person
A funny person

She is . . .
A smart person
A pretty person
Not a bad singer

She is . . .
A good reader
She cheers you up
A person who cares
Without hate
A person who loves

She is . . .
Loyal
Can keep a secret
Sometimes forgetful
Treats other people
Like she would want to be treated
She is . . .
Always truthful
Never stops loving you
Often loses her car keys

She is . . .
My mom.

Maddie

Brittany Smith
Thurman Francis Arts Academy, Grade 6

Maddie is my sister,
Sweet and cute is she,
But sometimes she can be somewhat of
A pain to me.
When I was just a little girl,
About five years old
"God, please give me a brother or sister,"
I told.
So then Mom had Maddie,
It happened when I was nine.
She was so cute and sweet,
But now she yells, "That's mine!"
Now she's two
Getting older by the year,
Sometimes she brings anger
Sometimes she brings cheer.
So that's Maddie for you,
Bad to the bone
Yet other times
She has the nicest, sweetest, cutest little tone.

Loved One

Penn Moore
Lascassas Elementary School, Grade 3

    My brother is the most amazing brother because of the way he shows me how to play sports. He also takes care of me. We play together some of the time. My grandfather teaches him something, and then my brother teaches it to me. We play each other in basketball, but he beats me anyway. But, it's still fun to play him. We get in fights, but he doesn't care. I look up to my brother. Whenever I get hurt, I look up. He's always the first one there. Whenever I get bossed around, he stands up for me. We play knee football in our den. He's the best brother you could have.

My Mother
Jeavonna Coble
Lascassas Elementary School, Grade 3

My mother is sweet as sugar. She always is there for me. When I'm mad or sad even when I'm glad she cheers me up. When I'm scared she kisses and hugs me. She buys me things that I really like. Everyone should know she is very nice. We do lots of things together, like play games and go see movies. My mom and I have the best time together but sometimes she can be mean. I still love my mom anyway. Sometimes I don't get attention but after that she becomes the best mom ever. Every day I think she is a star, the star of my life. She is more than anything in this whole universe to me and people should know how wonderful she is to me. She is a helpful, wonderful, lovable, and caring mother. I love you, Mom, very much.

Hero
Blake Adams-Manuel
Lascassas Elementary School, Grade 5

>
> Hero
> Nice, lovable
> Plays, laughs, sings
> He is my hero.
> Dad

I Believe I Can Fly
Katie L. Davis
Christiana Middle School, Grade 8

My dad sitting there all alone
Wishing his life was better
He doesn't know that I look up to him.
All of his mistakes have made me a better person.
He has taught me the better things in life.
Of how I can achieve anything
I believe it and go on trying
Knowing tomorrow is a better day
He has taught me that, too.
I love you, Dad.

Mom
Kalie Boyter
Lascassas Elementary School, Grade 5

>Mom
>Loving, kind
>Fun, cooks, tennis
>I love you bunches.
>Heather

Family Traditions
Joey Meier
Oakland High School, Grade 9

    The United States Army is very important and meaningful to my family and me. Not only does it protect, guard, and ensure the safety and well-being of our country and its citizens, but it has been a career that many of my family have chosen. Both of my grandfathers served in the Army, as well as two of my uncles.

    My dad's father, Pop-Pop, served during World War II. He was on the first wave of landing craft to arrive on Omaha Beach on D-Day. After his duty, he left the Army as a lieutenant. My mom's father, Grandpa, fought in both the Korean War and Vietnam War. He served as a helicopter pilot, transporting wounded soldiers. He retired from the Army as a colonel. Grandpa died of cancer last year, and he was buried at Arlington National Cemetery in Washington D.C. My Uncle Jeff served in the first Gulf War. He is a retired colonel. I was fortunate enough to attend his change of command at Fort Campbell, Kentucky. Before retiring, he was stationed at the Pentagon. My Uncle Steve fought in the Gulf War before leaving the Army as a major.

    I would love to follow in their footsteps and pursue a military career. I think it would be incredibly rewarding to protect our country and her people. The flag, which covered my grandfather's casket, has inspired me to consider a career in the Army. Before he was laid to rest, the Honor Guard folded the flag and gave it to my grandmother. His flag is kept at my grandmother's home in a special box designed to display flags. It serves as a reminder of how caring my grandfather was. When I see the flag, I think about how much he loved his country. I hope that someday I can personally experience the intense pride that he felt about being a part of the Army of One.

That Was for Grandpa
Justine Mettler
Christiana Middle School, Grade 8

Sometimes I sit back and remember those days
Sitting there beside him
My wonderful grandfather
He was always there
To tell me stories about his childhood
He always told me to go for my dreams
And never hold back
Give it my all
He was always there for me when I needed him the most
He told me that everything was all right
Until that tragic day
My mother got the phone call
Then she told me that everything was all right
We both knew she was lying
It has been seven years now
I will never forget his smile
Every time I accomplish one of my dreams
I know he is watching
It makes me proud to say,
"That was for you, Grandpa."

Times Spent with Grandma
Michael Pethke
Lascassas Elementary School, Grade 5

    My grandmother passed away two years ago. I miss her a lot. That's why she is my loved one. She used to let me drink coffee when I went to her house. She had three dogs. Two of them had puppies almost every seven months! I went to her house almost every weekend. I had at least two ticks on me because she lived right beside the woods. She had to be on a breathing machine because she smoked. That part, I didn't like. Every holiday, we spent at her house because she was alone. Christmas was the best time of the year because everybody went to her house. She was glad to be with the family. I think she was very glad to have us as grandchildren. I miss her with all my heart.

Clean Clothes
Brett Bloom
Christiana Middle School, Grade 8

Cleaned, dried, washed, and tumbled
Reminds me of my mother's smile
Twisted and spun during her troubles
But fixed and folded in a little while
Little stains will always stay
And affect the outlook forever more
When pulled from the turmoil,
It doesn't matter; she overcomes it evermore
Deaths and births, living and dying
She's been through it all
Like a cotton shirt out to dry.

Something I Did in Japan
Yoshimi Kajisa
Roy Waldron School, Grade 3

On summer vacation, we went to Japan to meet our grandma and grandpa. I was nervous about it. I hated to go on the train and plane. It was cool when we looked out of the windows. The cars looked like tiny ants that were moving slowly. We went out of the plane and then we went on the train. We had to ride on a train and plane. Next we were there. We had fun. We went to a lot of pools and our grandma and grandpa bought us a lot of things. We stayed there for sixty days. Maybe we stayed there about forty days. And then we went to our Dad's grandma and grandpa. Finally, our mom and dad came. My mom came back from Korea and my Dad came back, too. Our family was back together. We did a lot of fun things together. My brother, sister, and I had friends. We went to the beach. We did too many things there. And later, we went back to America. I think I like Japan better then America. But I think that I like America.

Granny
Ally Eaton
Buchanan Elementary School, Grade 6

I loved her
And I wonder
Where she went after that
All I know is that she liked hats
I loved her
And I wonder
Where she went after that.

In memory of
Jane Byrum Langston

Love and Limitations
Kelsey Caffy
Oakland High School, Grade 9

Both of you were chosen for me
To care, to raise and to love
To show me what is right and wrong
You gave me a place to belong.

When I was younger, I did not understand your rules
Why could I never jump on the couch?
Why could I never stay home alone?
Do I have to wait for everything until I am grown?

Now, at fifteen, I am still a little confused.
Why can I never watch R-rated movies?
What is wrong with leaving my clothes on the floor?
I do not want to study or do homework anymore.

Do not worry, though, I am beginning to get it.
I appreciate each of you more every day;
I am starting to understand and see.
I am making connections between rules and your love for me!

Acknowledgements

Special thanks to all the teachers who helped make this project a success

Barfield Elementary School
Sunita Watson

Blackman Elementary School
Latasha Allison
Tammy Anselmo
Libby Black
Valori Bond
Wendy Davenport
Melanie Fitzgerald
Sandy Graves
Catherine Herbert
Melnequa Holloway
Kelly Jones
Kenda Lynch
Brenda Martin
Tisonya Mastin
Deborah Maxwell
Ray Ann McCord
Pam Morgan
Dina Nave
Emily Osbourn
Angela Pope
Angelia Smith
Marcella Watts
Tina Whitfield
Connie Wiel
Wanda Wiggs
April Williams
Fannie Williams
Ashley Witt
Kerri Womack
Robin Wood

Blackman Middle School
Paige Barber
Leisa Barrier
June Culp
Jeff Harding
Nicole Hurt
Marcie Leeman
Beverly McGee

Buchanan Elementary School
Vzea Foster

Cedar Grove Elementary School
Sonya Cox
Melissa Greer

Central Middle School
Carol Berning

Christiana Elementary School
Kathleen Davis

Christiana Middle School
Kenneth Cooper
Lisa Ezell
Barbara Powers

David Youree Elementary School
Bobby Duke
Jerri McKee
Darnette Merriweather

Eagleville School
Melissa Broyles
Retika Dial
Theresa Hill
Melissa Mankin

Holloway High School
Kilby Watson

Homer Pittard Campus School
Helen Babb
Cary Holman

Lascassas Elementary School
Jennifer Chattin
Krista Denton
Karen Horne
Pat Ingle
Melissa Kincaid
Kim Lochmondy
JoLyn McWhorter
Kristi Peay
Vanessa Tipton
Mary Beth Walkup

LaVergne Middle School
Andrea Duncan
Paige Hawkins
Elizabeth Wood

LaVergne Primary School
Mary Powers

McFadden School of Excellence
Debra Brown
Christa Campbell
Stacey Conatser
Lisa Elliott
Lilly Large
Nancy Levi
Debra Lyles
Lark Petty
Sally Whittenburg

Oakland High School
Karen Cox
Jim Gifford
Chris Hudson
Nancy Jackson
Mary Sue Persons
Diane Wade

Riverdale High School
Barbara Collie
Maxine Gaither

Rockvale Elementary School
Carol Burns
Kerri Clark
Marcy Pflueger

Rock Springs Middle School
April Sneed
Kelly Young

Roy Waldron School
Linda Hagan
Paige Johnson
Melanie Jones
Cheryl Marshall
Mel Prater

Siegel High School
Kim Cing
Karen Garner
Patricia Morgan
Kelli Nichols
Myra O'Steen
Steve York

Siegel Middle School
Gloria Nolan

Smyrna Elementary School
D'ann Cooper
Tonya Hollandsworth
Diane Moore

Smyrna High School
Rebecca Robertson
Jill Walls

Smyrna Primary School
Reta Barney
Christa Brown
Jennifer Dowell
Kristina Maddux
Jennifer Monroe
Cynthia Roberts

Smyrna West Alternative School
Elizabeth Jennings
Kara Porter

Thurman Francis Arts Academy
Ginger Adcock
Nancy Essary
Kaye Ganoe
Janelle Gehrke
Susan Loveless
Jane Macomber
Shannon Marlin
Diane McElroy
Marilla Naron
Janie Reeder
Elizabeth Schurger
Amelie Sharp
Karen Smith
Tracy Townes
Allison Warren
Brian Wilcox

Walter Hill Elementary School

Emily Baker
Teresa Brockwell
Karen Burrell
Beverly Carlton
Cheryl Cotham
Jean Duncan
Betty Hodgin
Susan Pawlowski
Cassie Urban
Lynn Womack

Wilson Elementary School

Kate Campbell
Jennifer Clifton
Caren Davis
Ann Haley
Kenya Howse
Lisa Kegler
Cindy McCreery
Holly Ray
Judy Templeton
Patti Todd